W9-AAW-237

JIMMY SNIFFLES DOGNAPPED!

Librarian Reviewer
Laurie K. Holland
Media Specialist (National Board Certified), Edina, MN
MA in Elementary Education, Minnesota State University, Mankato

Reading Consultant
Mark DeYoung
Classroom Teacher, Edina Public Schools, MN
BA in Elementary Education, Central College
MS in Curriculum & Instruction, University of Minnesota

STONE ARCH BOOKS
MINNEAPOLIS SAN DIEGO

Graphic Sparks are published by Stone Arch Books,
A Capstone Imprint
151 Good Counsel Drive, P.O. Box 669
Mankato, Minnesota 56002
www.capstonepub.com

Library of Congress Cataloging-in-Publication Data
Nickel, Scott.
    Dognapped! / by Scott Nickel; illustrated by Steve Harpster.
    p. cm. — (Graphic Sparks. Jimmy Sniffles)
    ISBN-13: 978-1-59889-053-2 (library binding)
    ISBN-10: 1-59889-053-0 (library binding)
    ISBN-13: 978-1-59889-226-0 (paperback)
    ISBN-10: 1-59889-226-6 (paperback)
    1. Graphic novels. I. Harpster, Steve. II. Title. III. Series.
PN6727.N544J56 2007
741.5'973—dc22   2006007698

Summary: Jimmy Sniffles' super-schnozz smells trouble when the neighborhood dogs begin
to disappear. A creepy clown and a lady with big hair are making a secret circus with the
missing mutts. Only Jimmy and his nose can save the day!

Art Director: Heather Kindseth
Graphic Designer: Keegan Gilbert

Printed in the United States of America in Stevens Point, Wisconsin
052010
005774R

JIMMY SNIFFLES DOGNAPPED!

BY SCOTT NICKEL

ILLUSTRATED BY STEVE HARPSTER

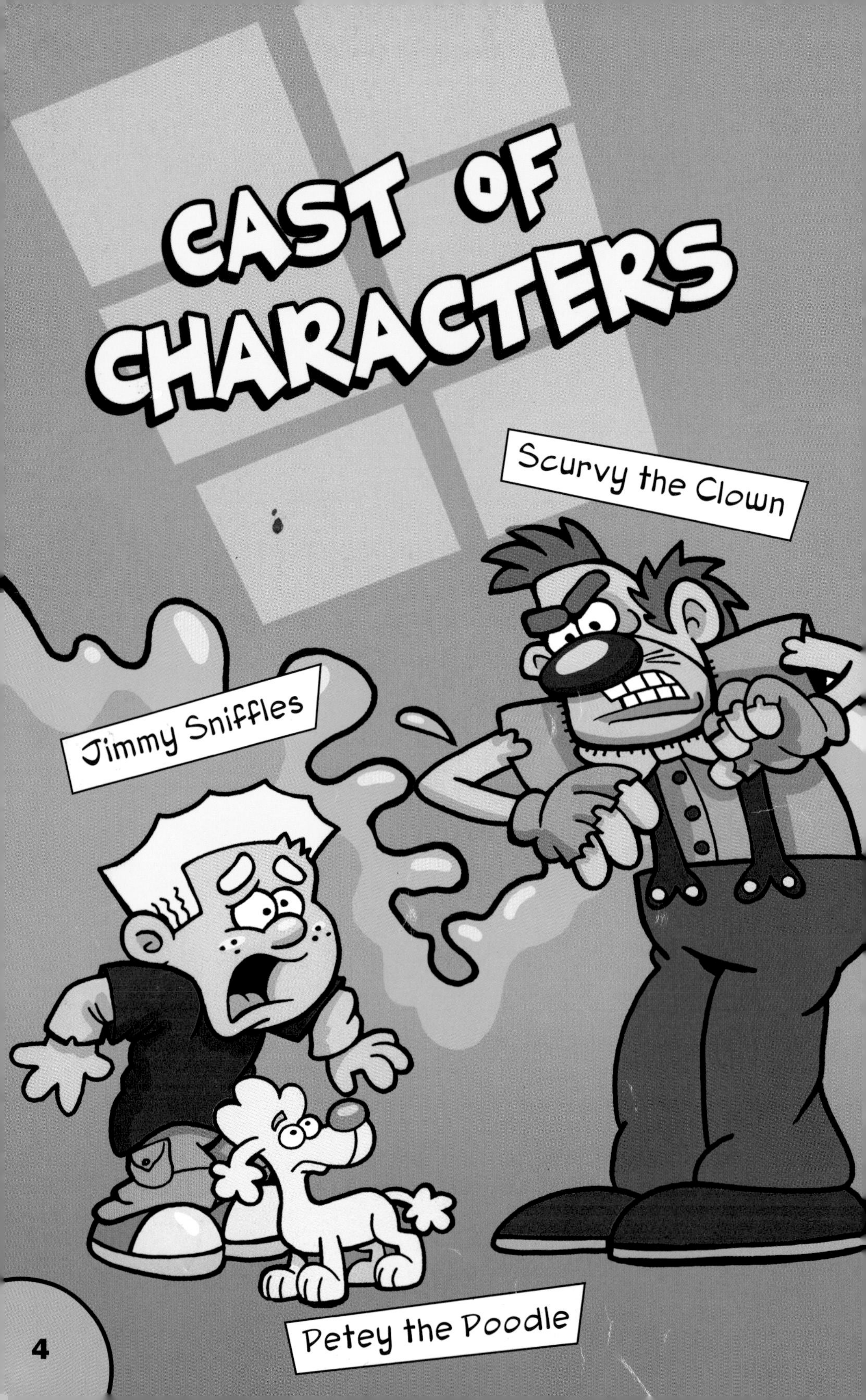
CAST OF CHARACTERS
Scurvy the Clown
Jimmy Sniffles
Petey the Poodle

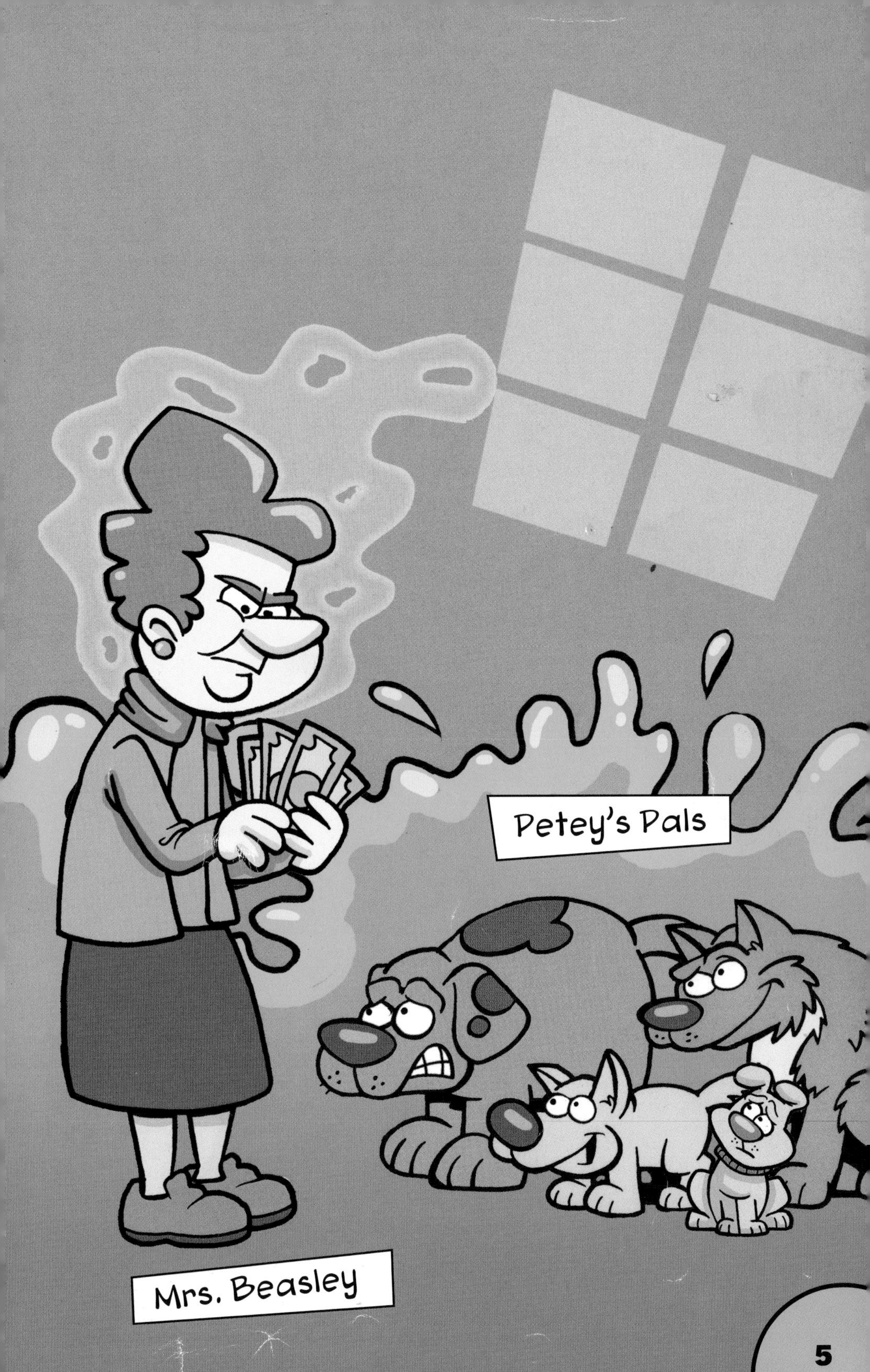
Petey's Pals
Mrs. Beasley

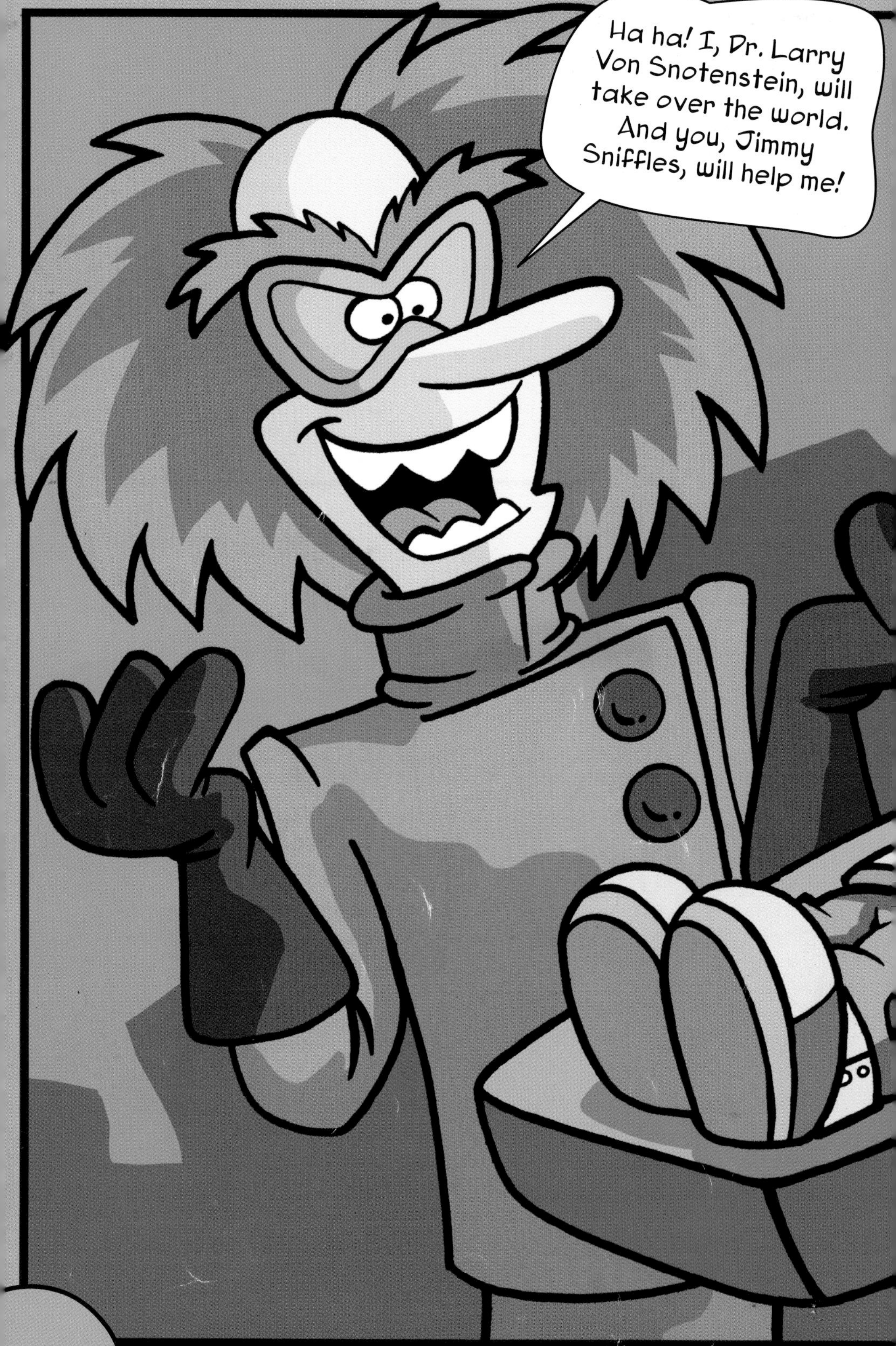
Ha ha! I, Dr. Larry Von Snotenstein, will take over the world. And you, Jimmy Sniffles, will help me!

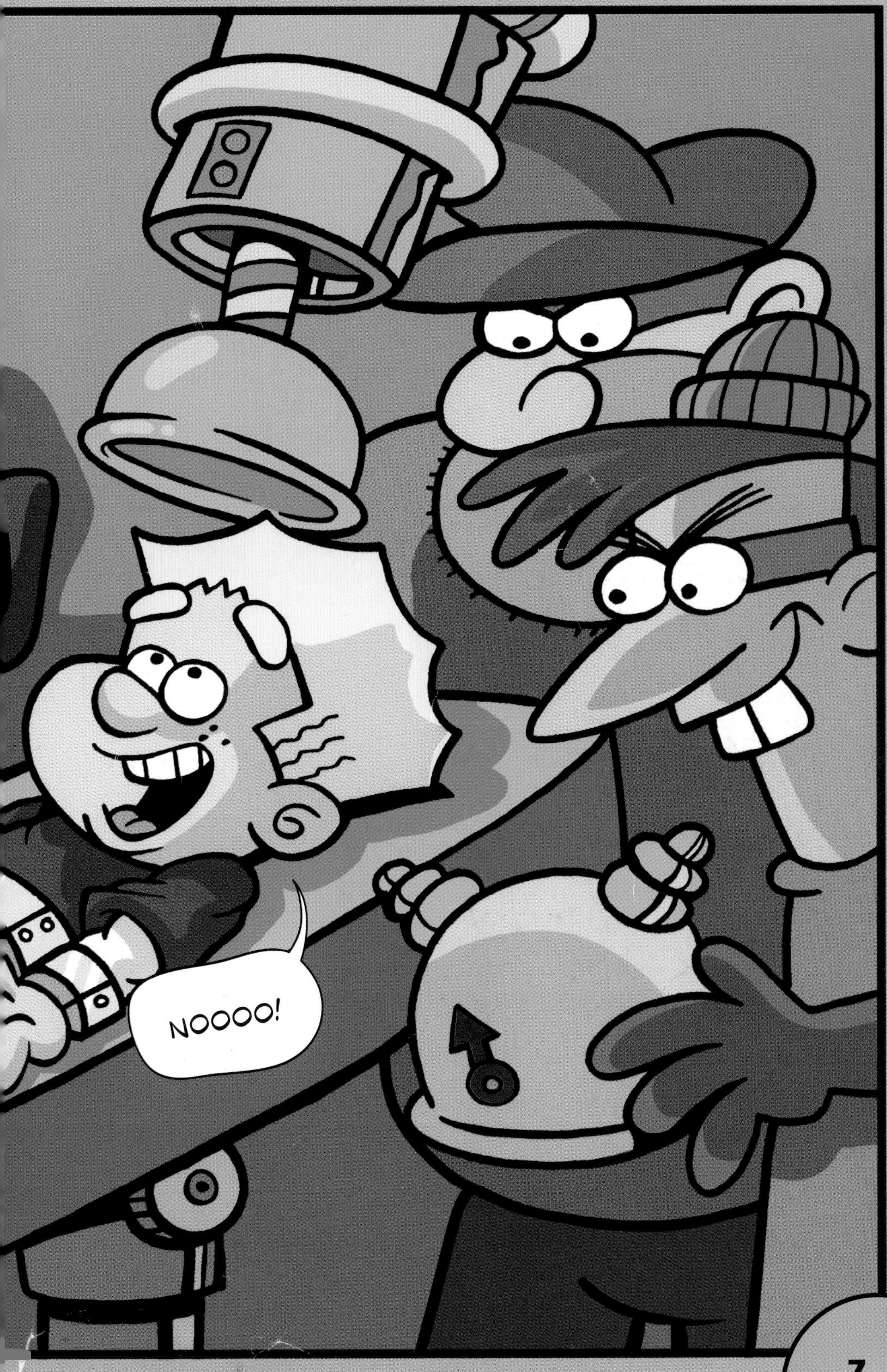
NOOOO!

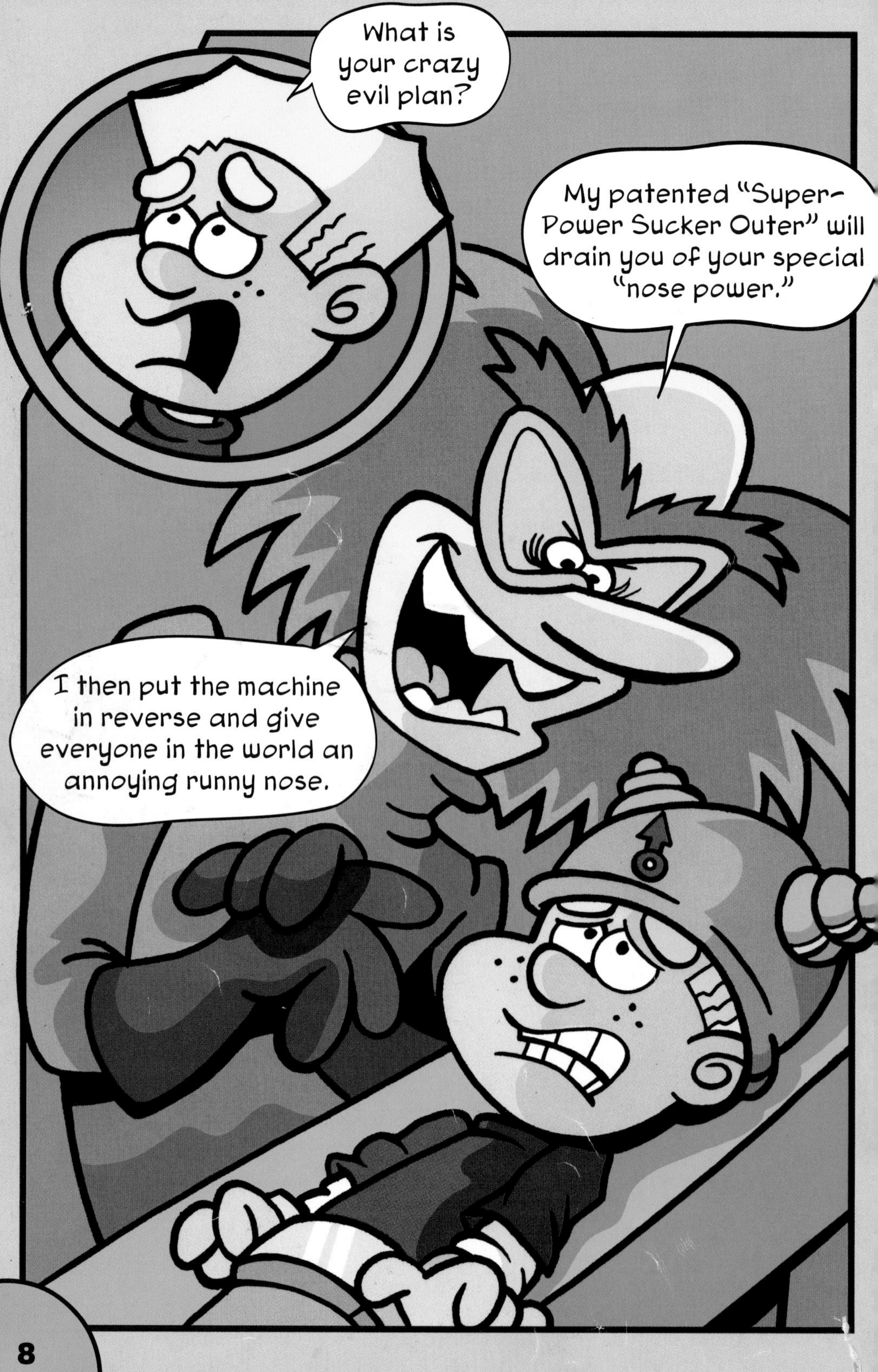
What is your crazy evil plan?
My patented "Super-Power Sucker Outer" will drain you of your special "nose power."
I then put the machine in reverse and give everyone in the world an annoying runny nose.

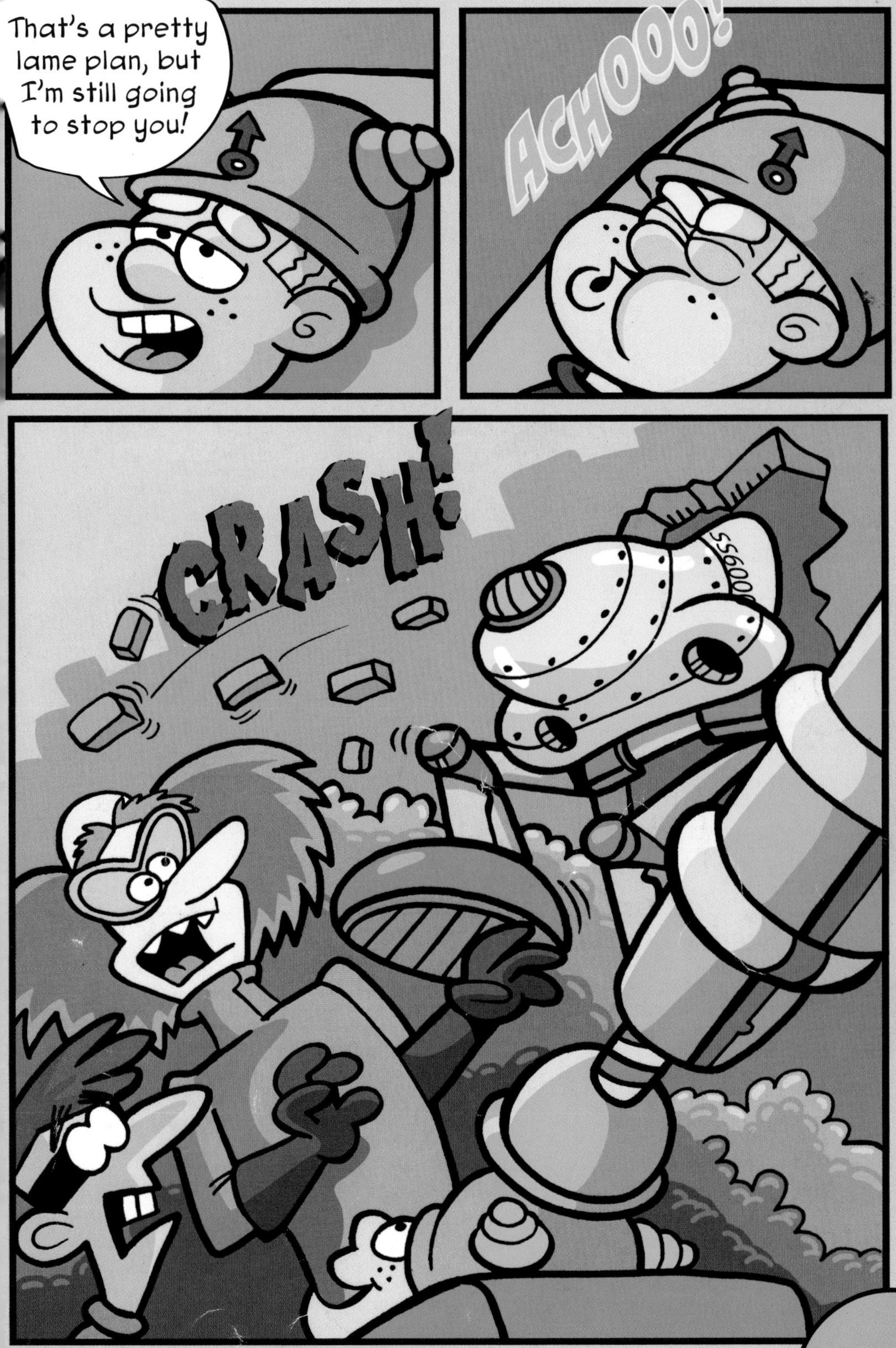
That's a pretty lame plan, but I'm still going to stop you!
ACHOOO!
CRASH!

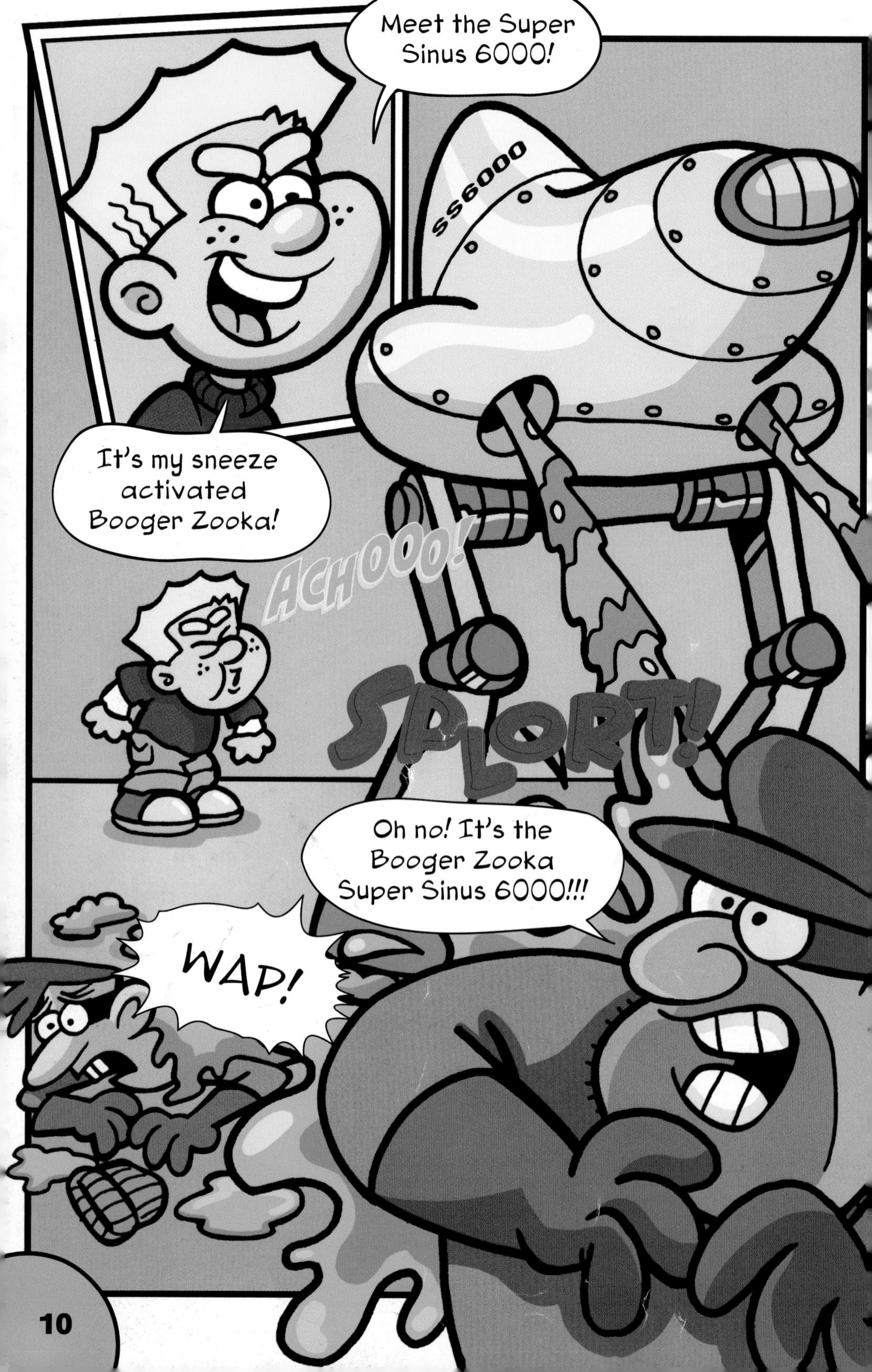
Meet the Super Sinus 6000!
SS6000
It's my sneeze activated Booger Zooka!
ACHOOO!
SPLORT!
Oh no! It's the Booger Zooka Super Sinus 6000!!!
WAP!

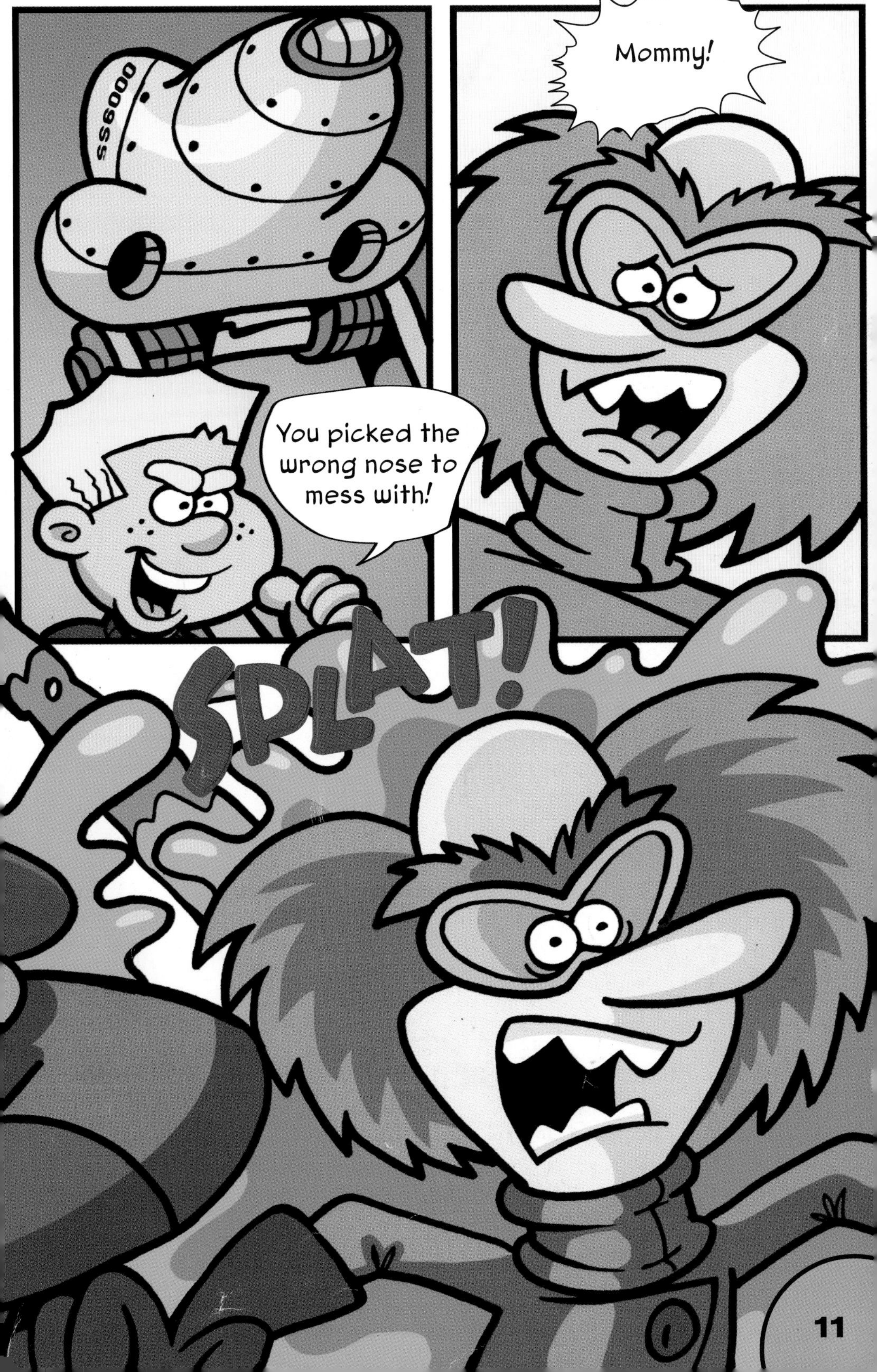

You picked the wrong nose to mess with!
SS6000
Mommy!
SPLAT!

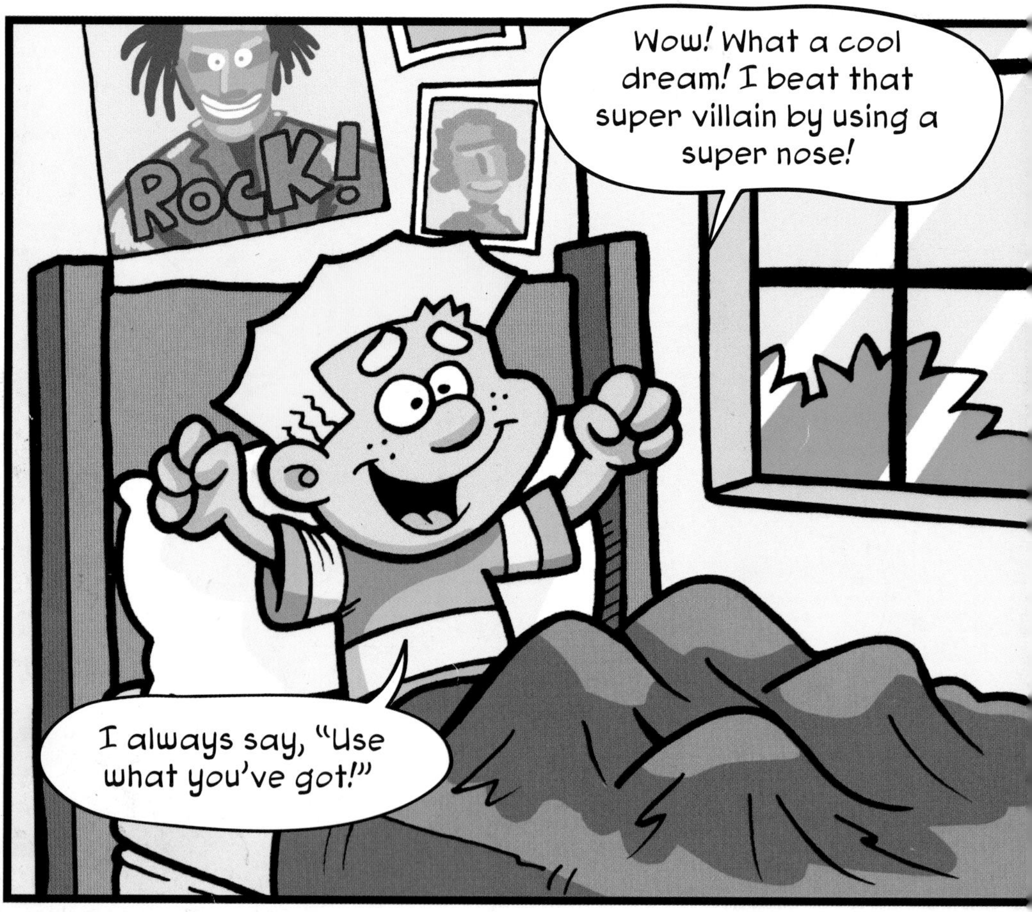
ROCK!
Wow! What a cool dream! I beat that super villain by using a super nose!
I always say, "Use what you've got!"

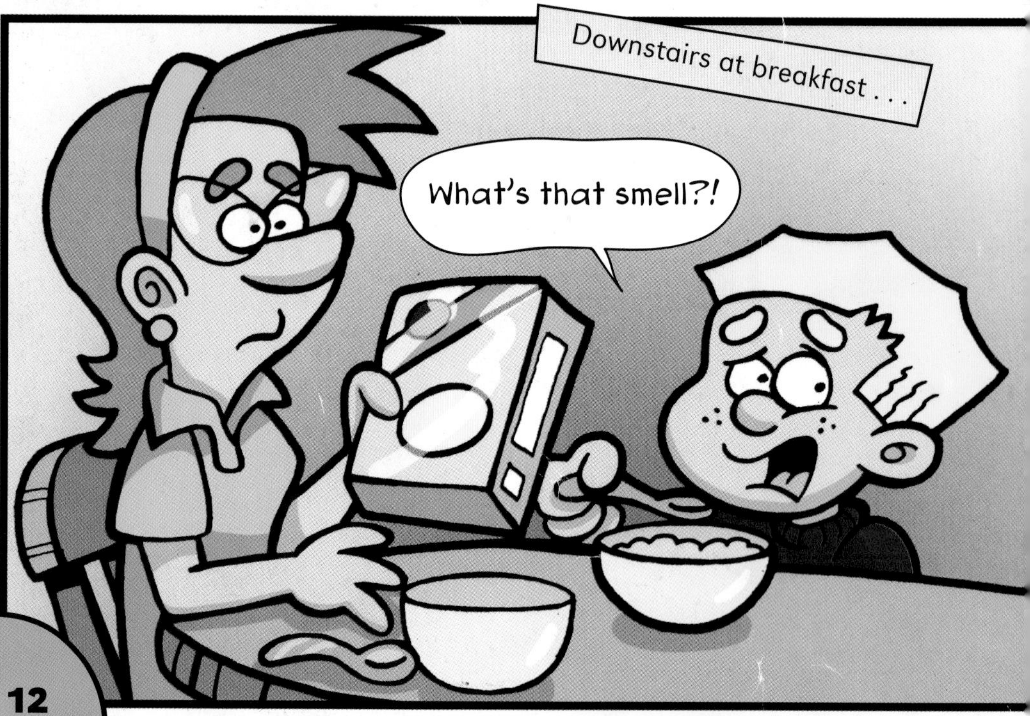
Downstairs at breakfast . . .
What's that smell?!

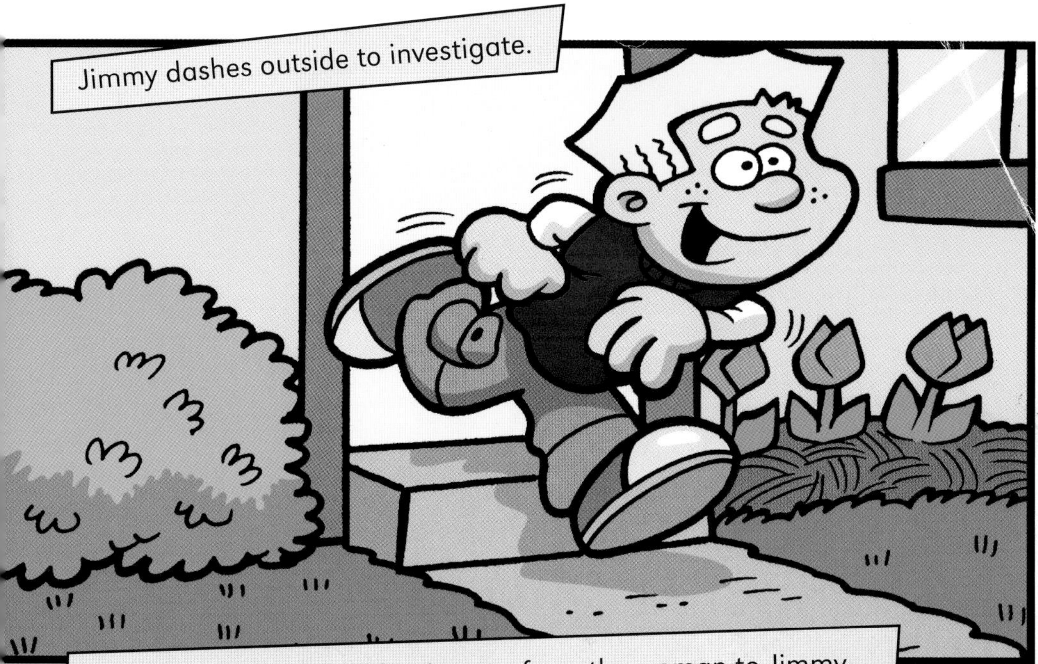
Jimmy dashes outside to investigate.

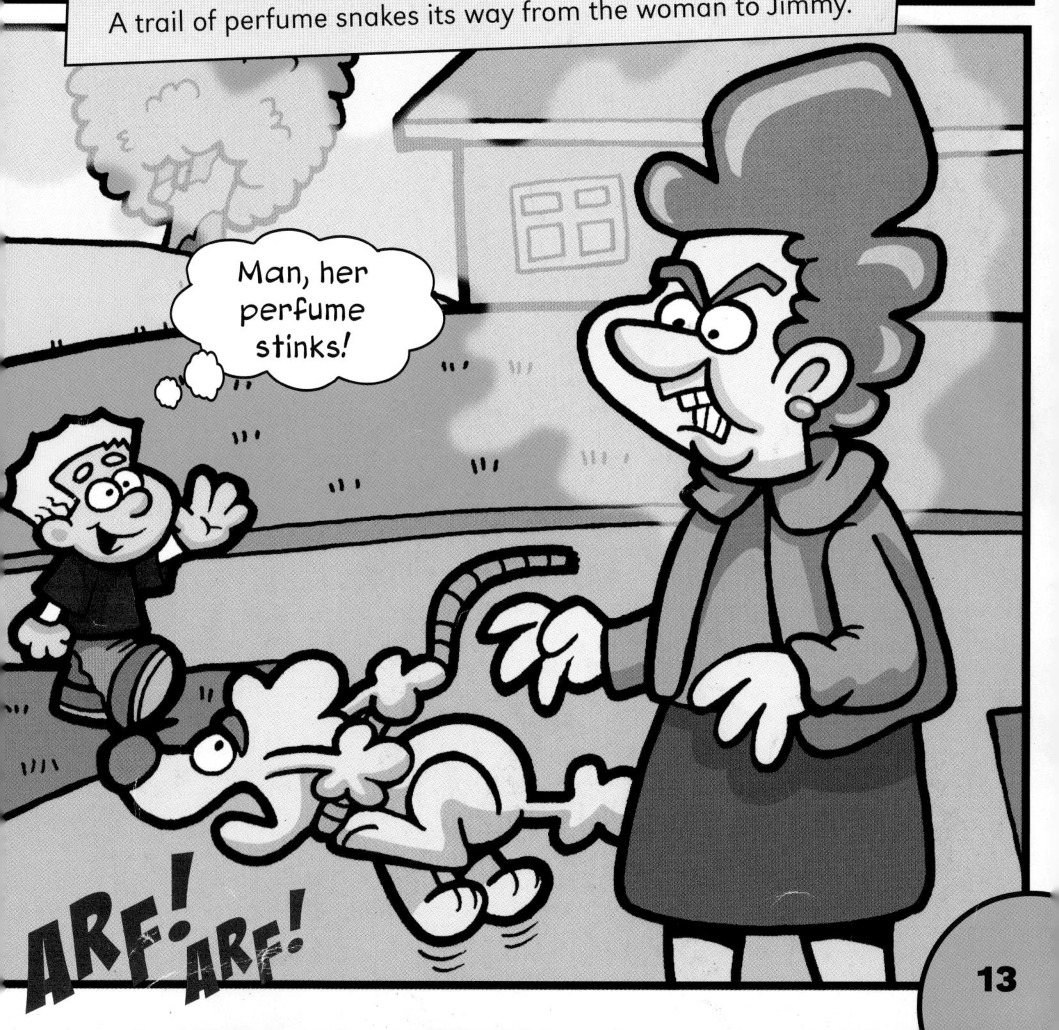
A trail of perfume snakes its way from the woman to Jimmy.
Man, her perfume stinks!
ARF! ARF!

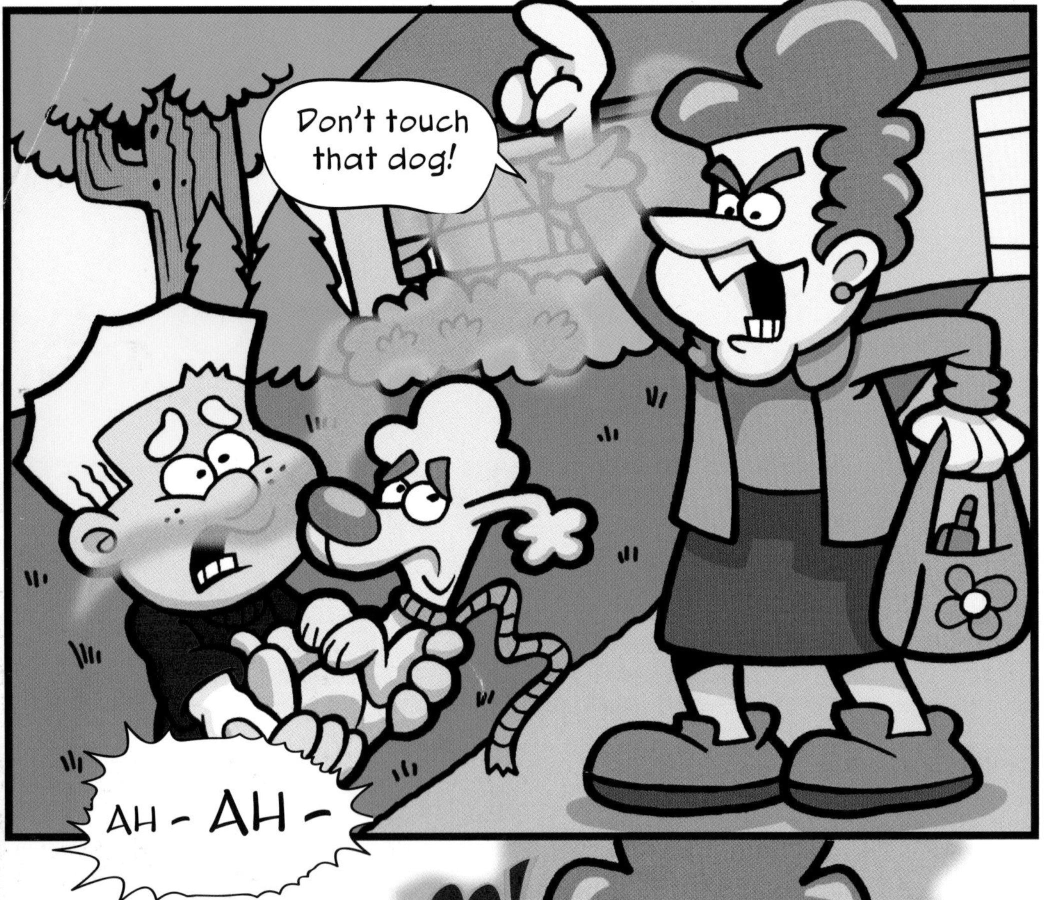
Don't touch
that dog!
AH - AH -

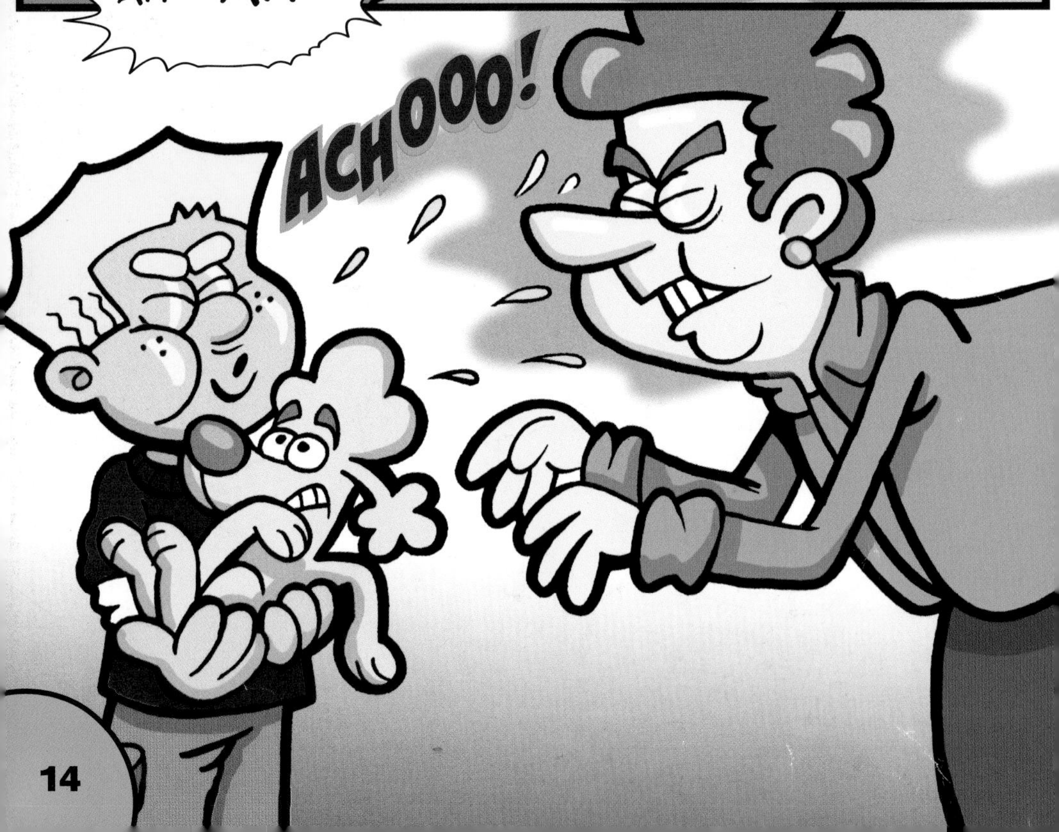
ACHOOO!

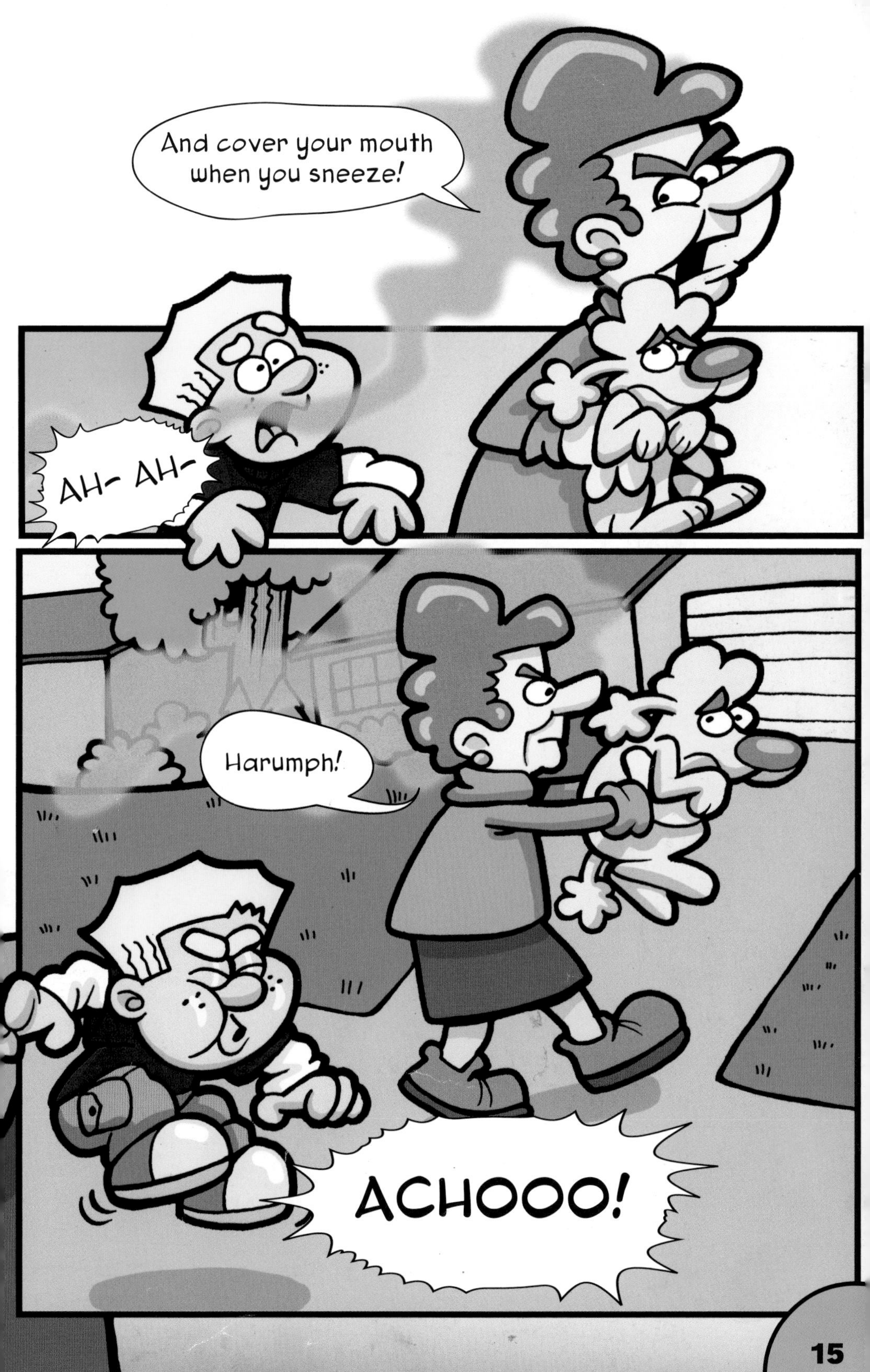

And cover your mouth when you sneeze!
AH- AH-
Harumph!
ACHOOO!

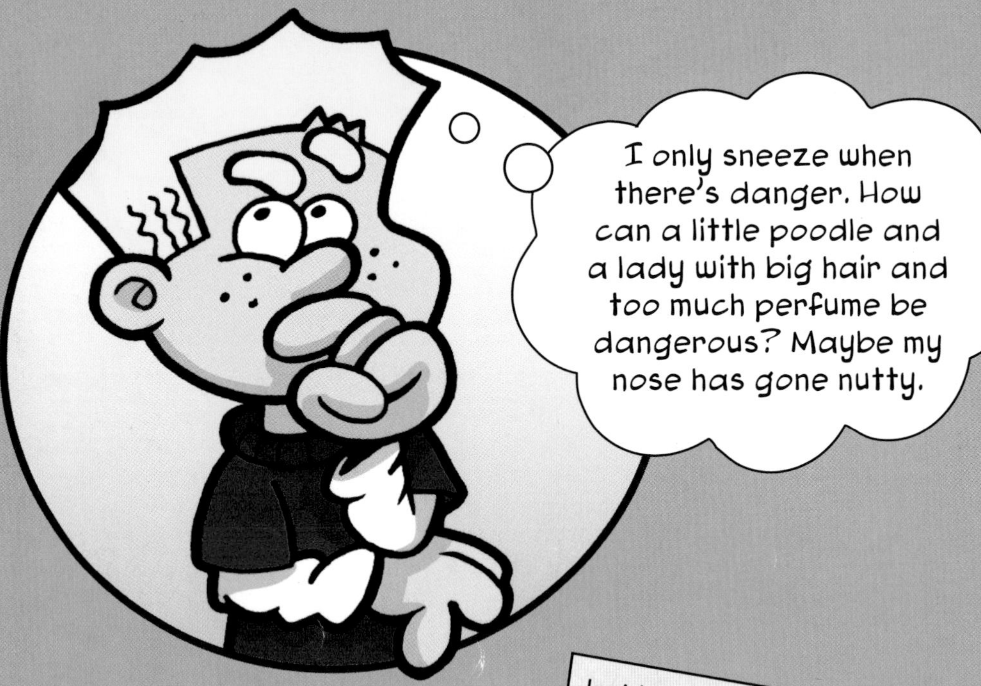
I only sneeze when there's danger. How can a little poodle and a lady with big hair and too much perfume be dangerous? Maybe my nose has gone nutty.

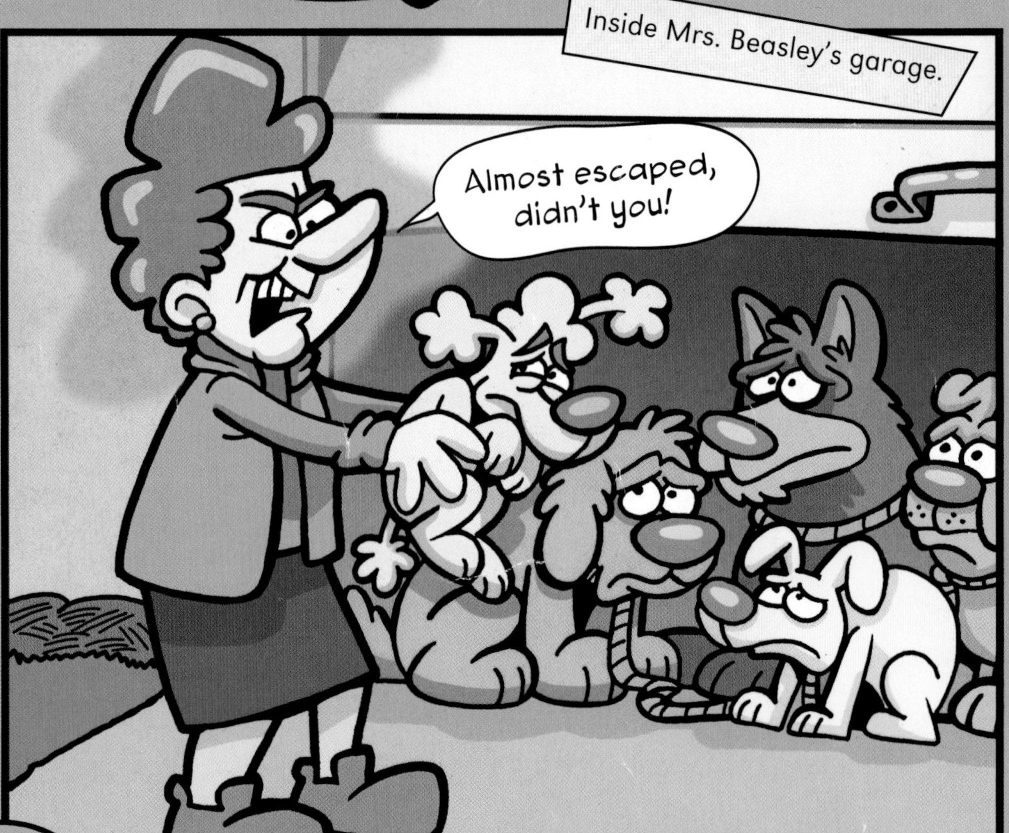
Inside Mrs. Beasley's garage.
Almost escaped, didn't you!

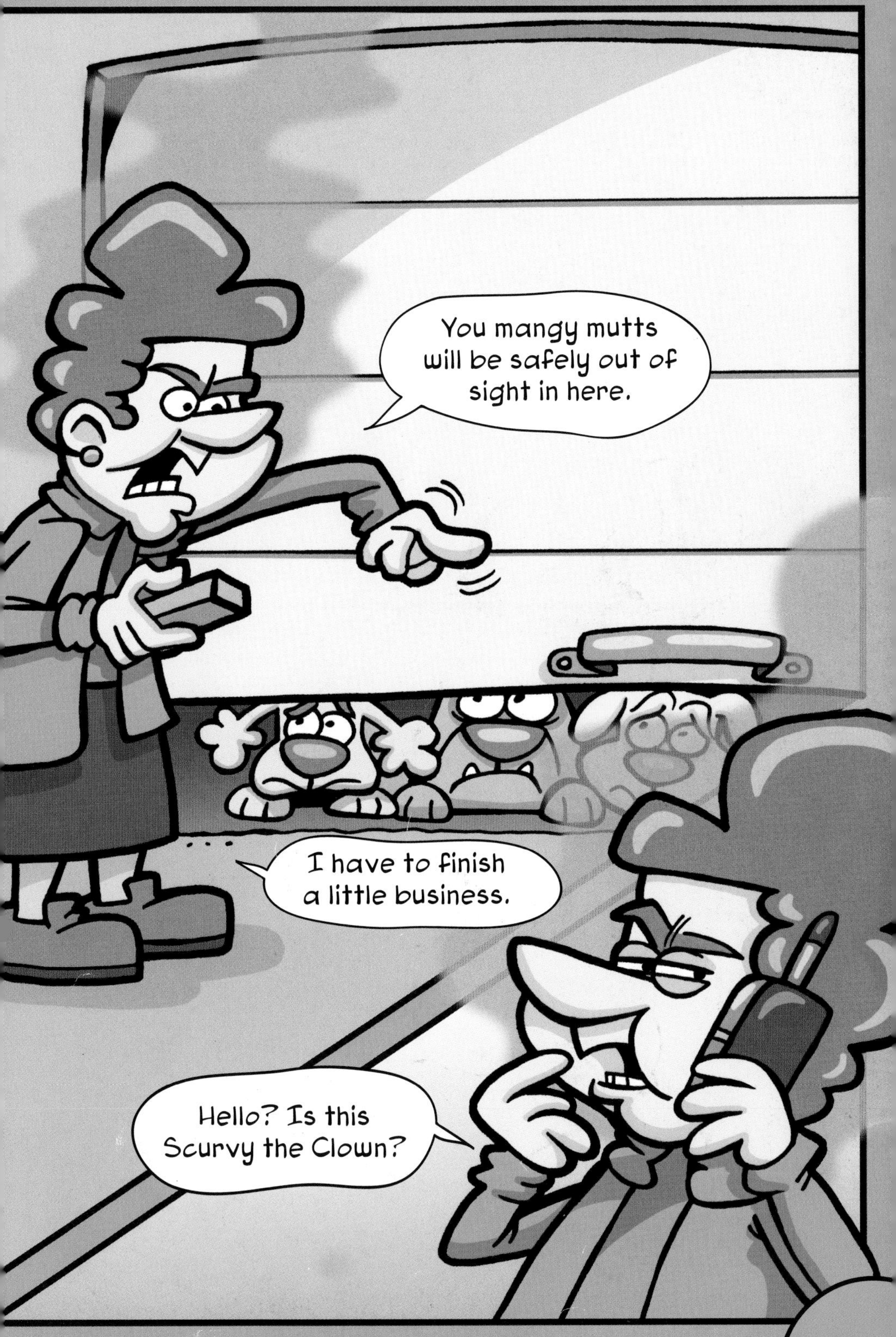
You mangy mutts will be safely out of sight in here.
I have to finish a little business.
Hello? Is this Scurvy the Clown?

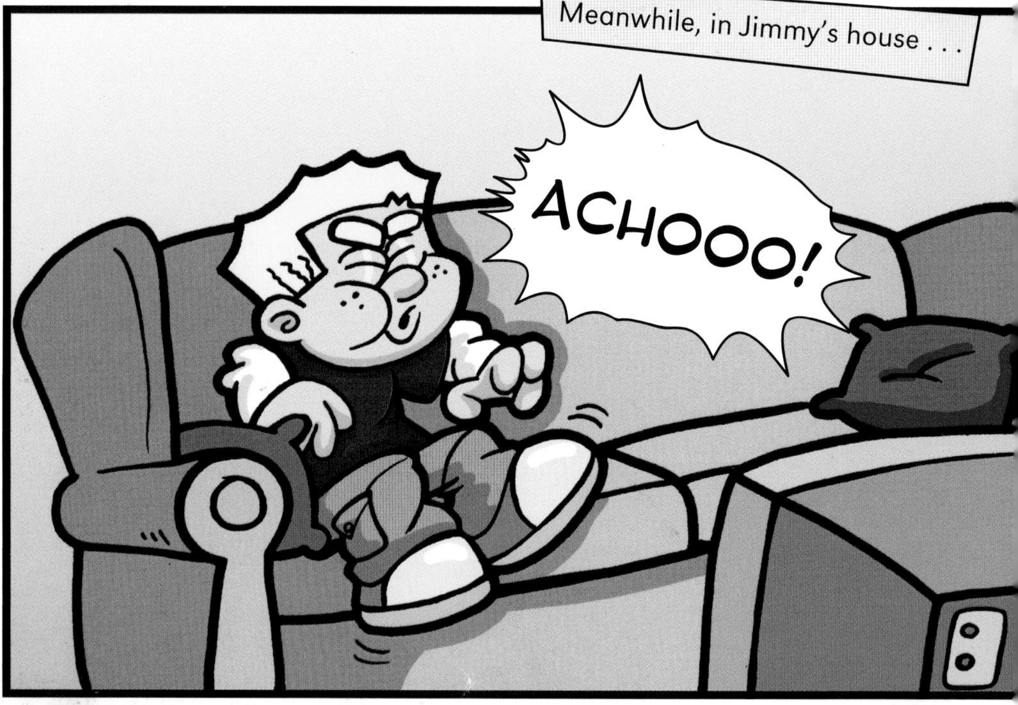
Meanwhile, in Jimmy's house . . .
ACHOOO!

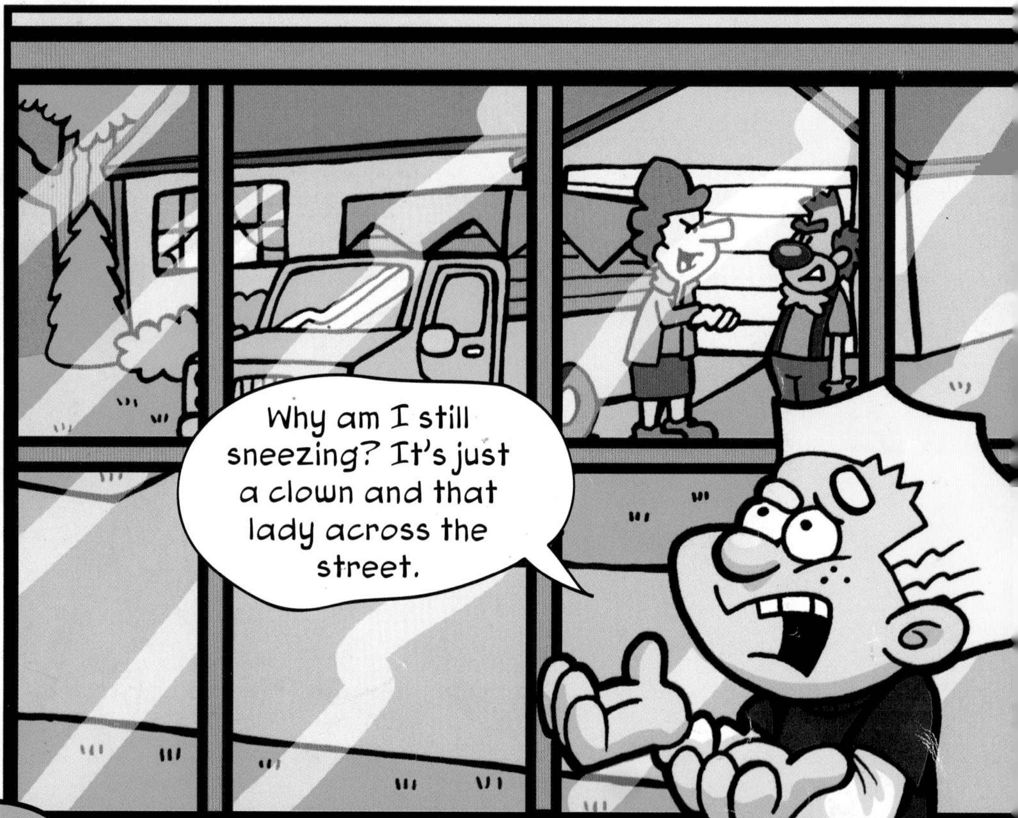
Why am I still sneezing? It's just a clown and that lady across the street.

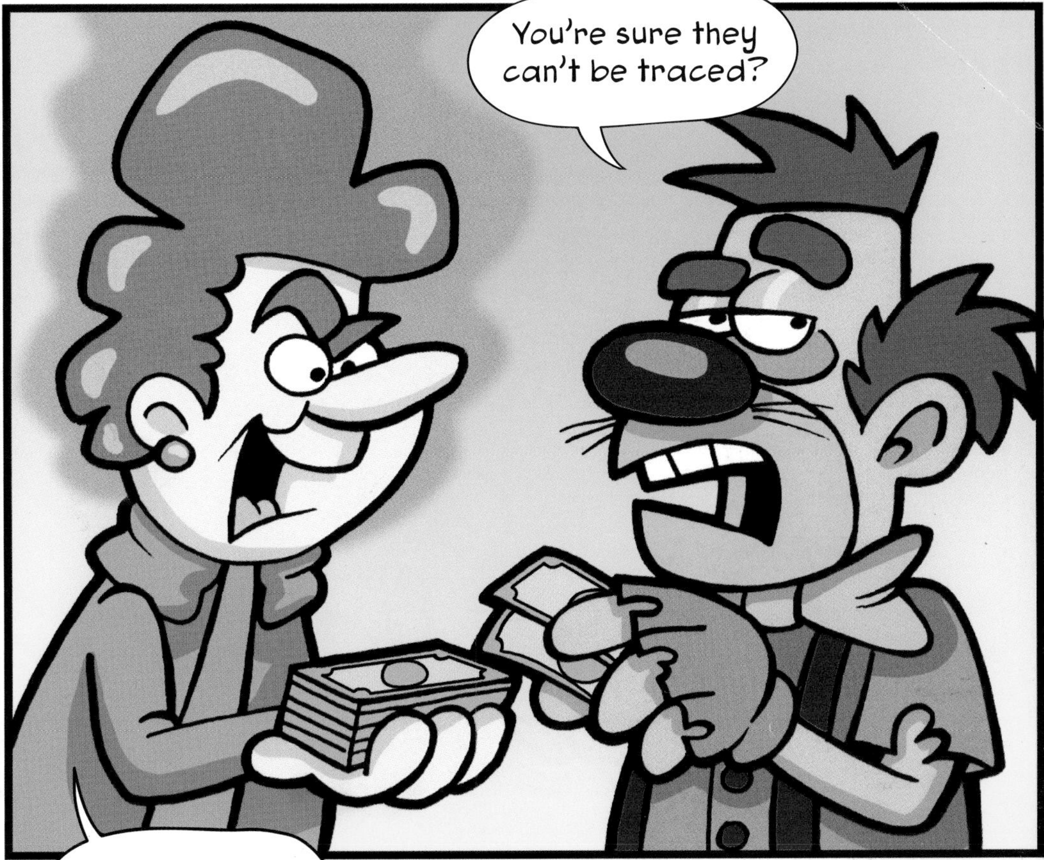
You're sure they can't be traced?
I took off all their collars.

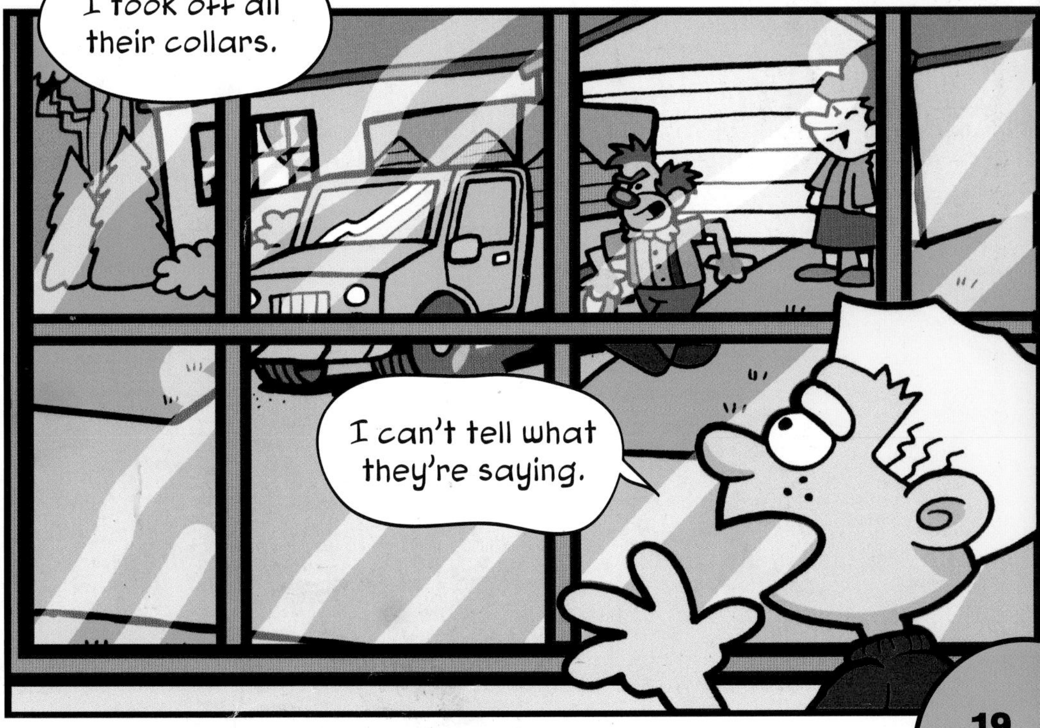
I can't tell what they're saying.

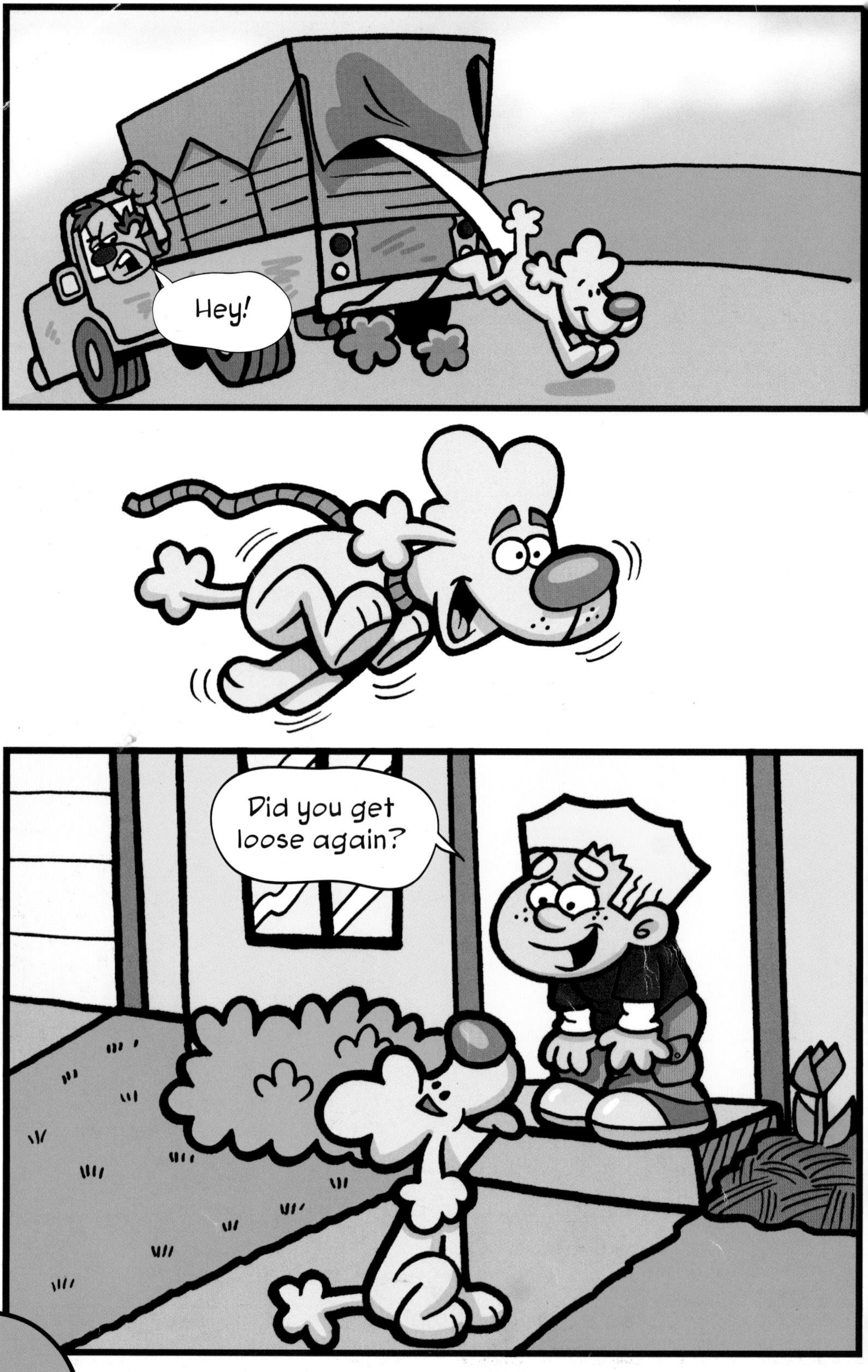
Hey!
Did you get loose again?

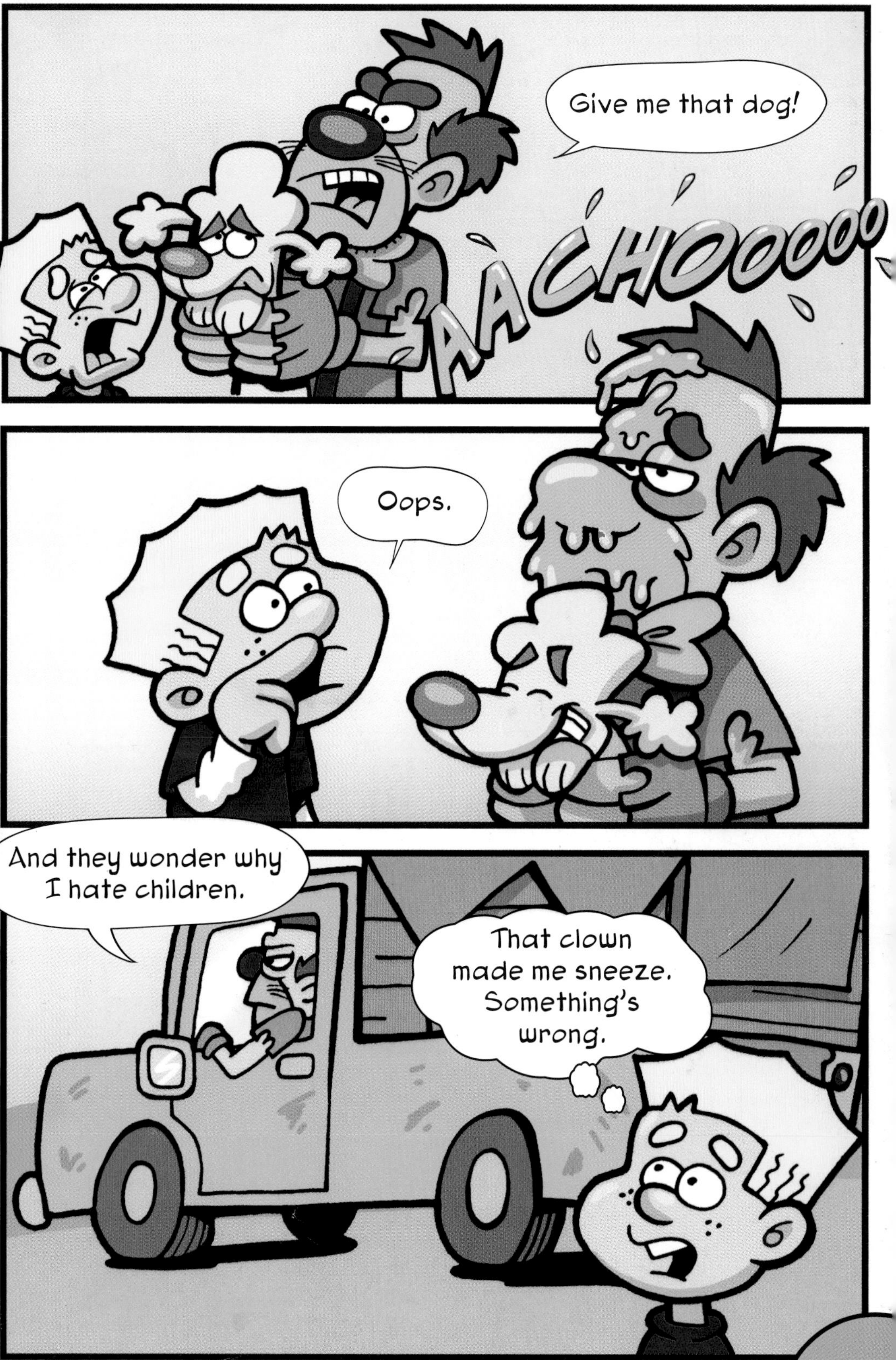
Give me that dog!
AACHOOOOOO
Oops.
And they wonder why I hate children.
That clown made me sneeze. Something's wrong.

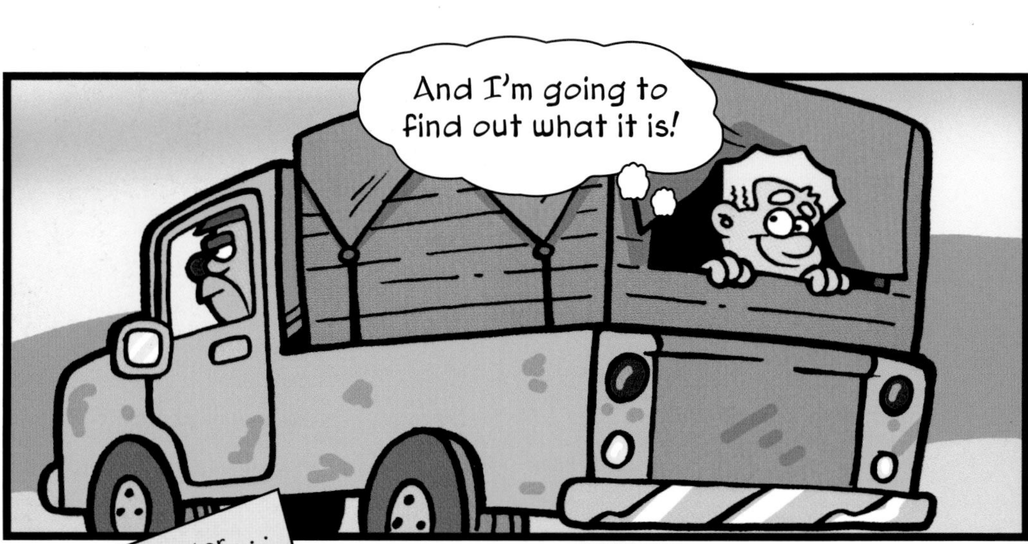
And I'm going to find out what it is!

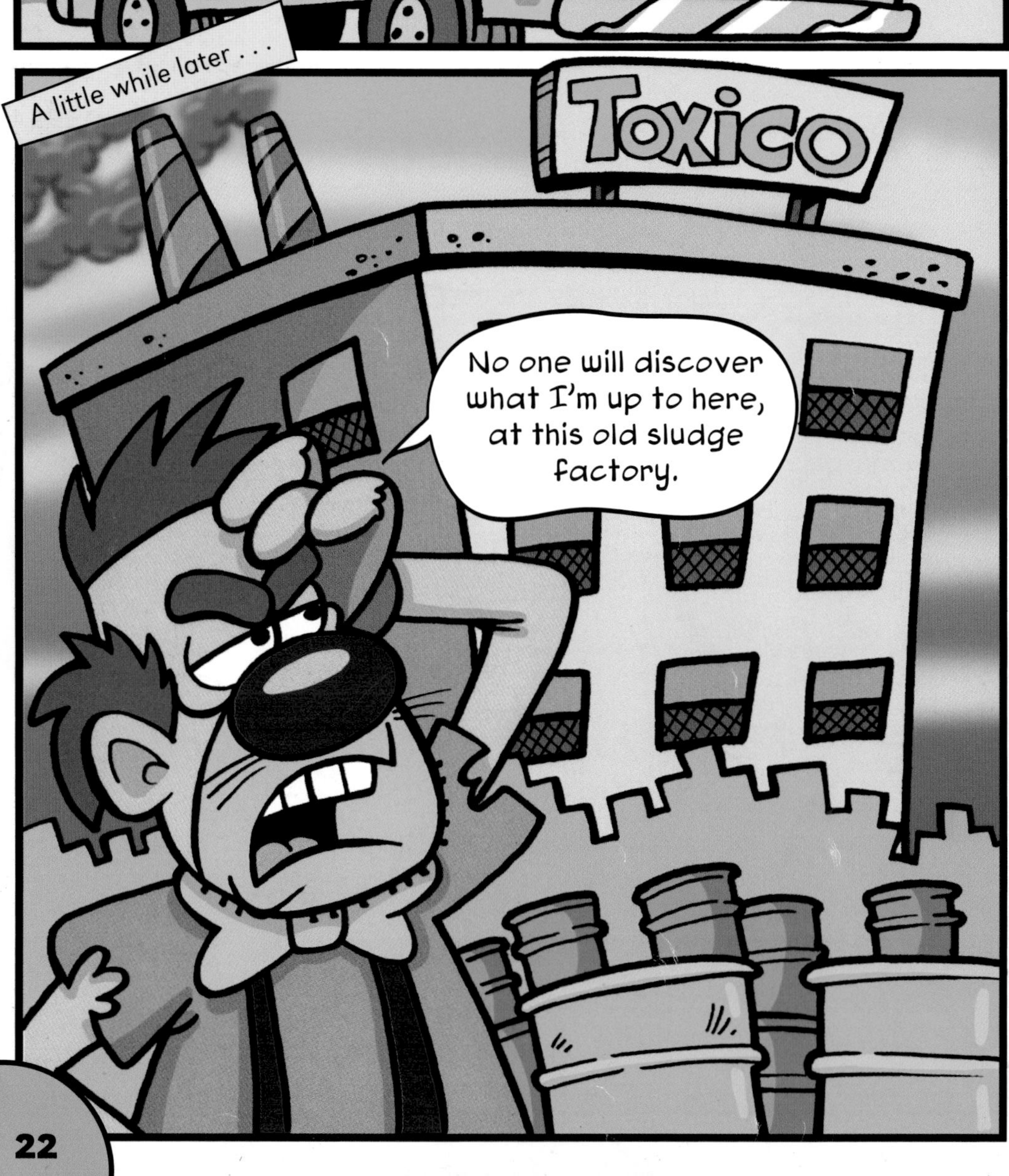
A little while later . . .
TOXICO
No one will discover what I'm up to here, at this old sludge factory.

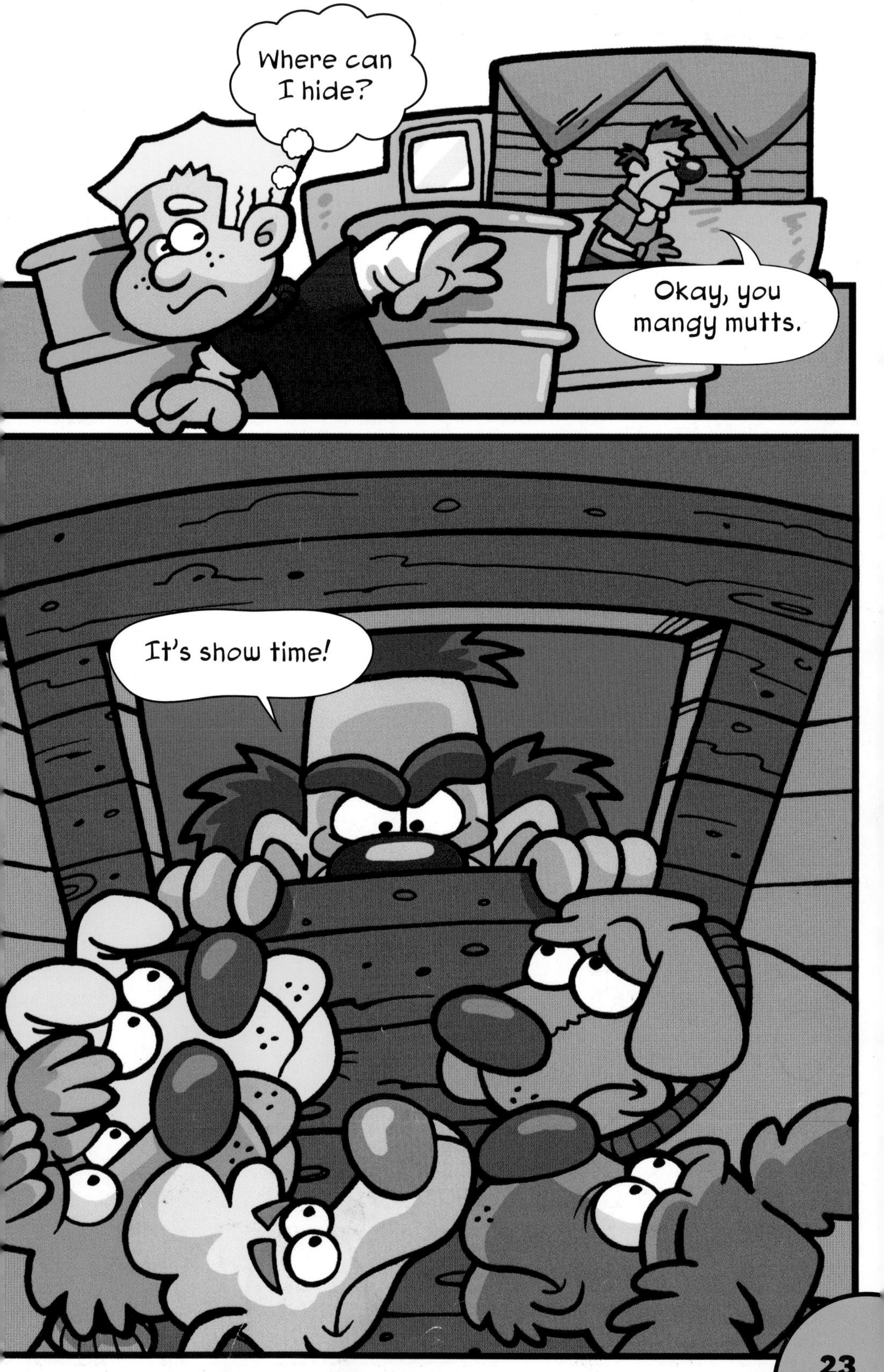
Where can I hide?
Okay, you mangy mutts.
It's show time!

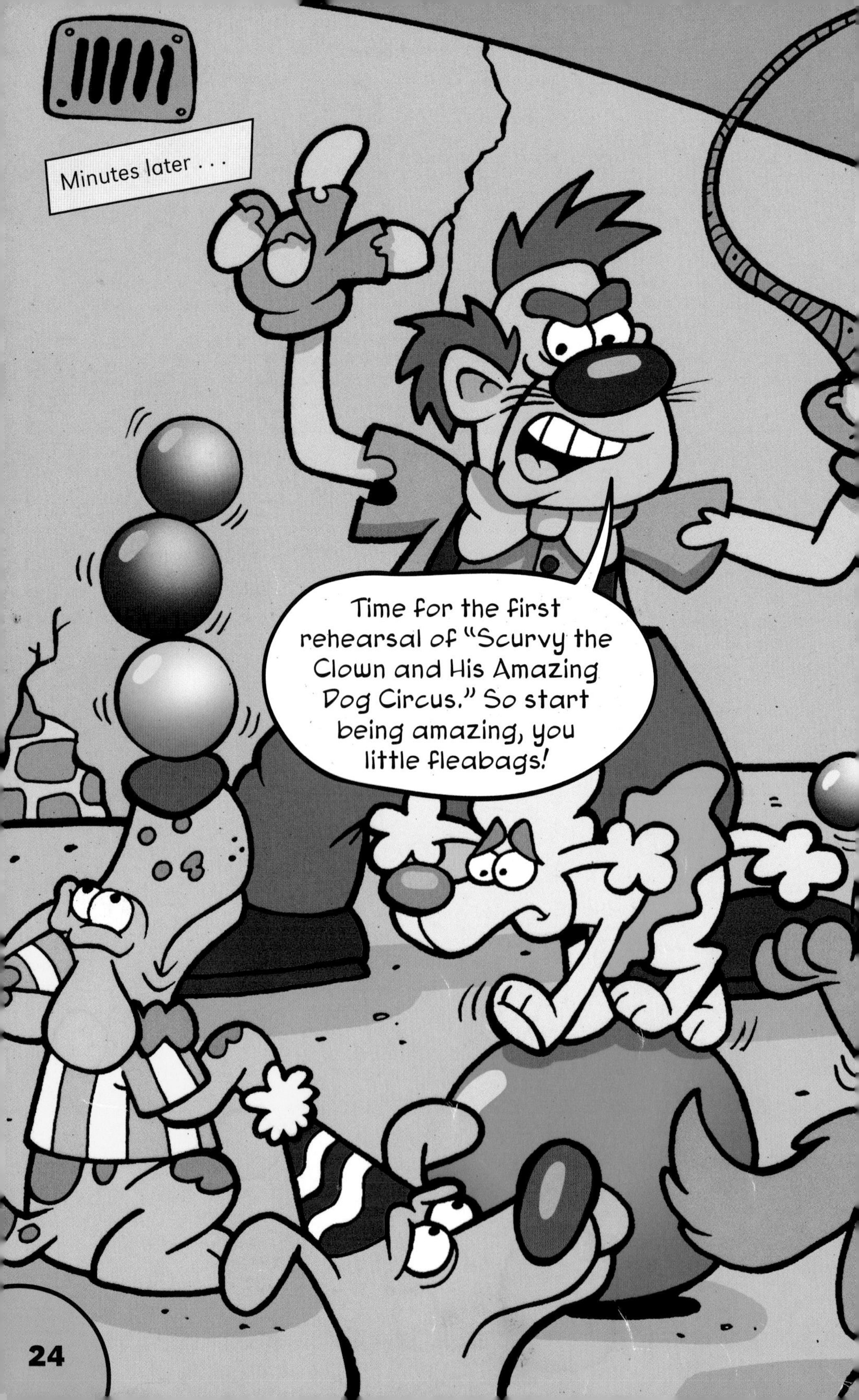
Minutes later . . .
Time for the first rehearsal of "Scurvy the Clown and His Amazing Dog Circus." So start being amazing, you little fleabags!

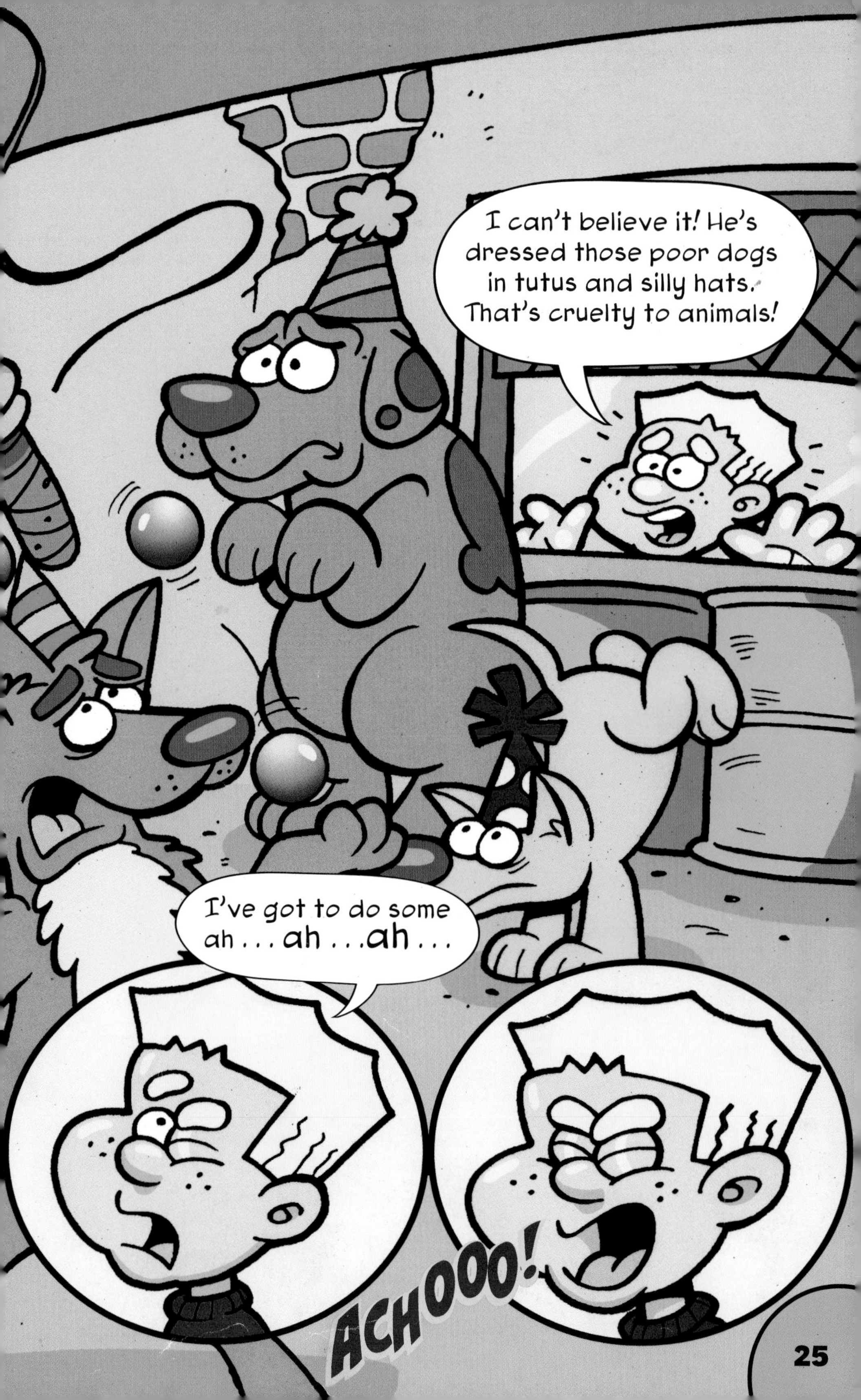
I can't believe it! He's dressed those poor dogs in tutus and silly hats. That's cruelty to animals!
I've got to do some ah . . . ah . . . ah . . .
ACHOOO!

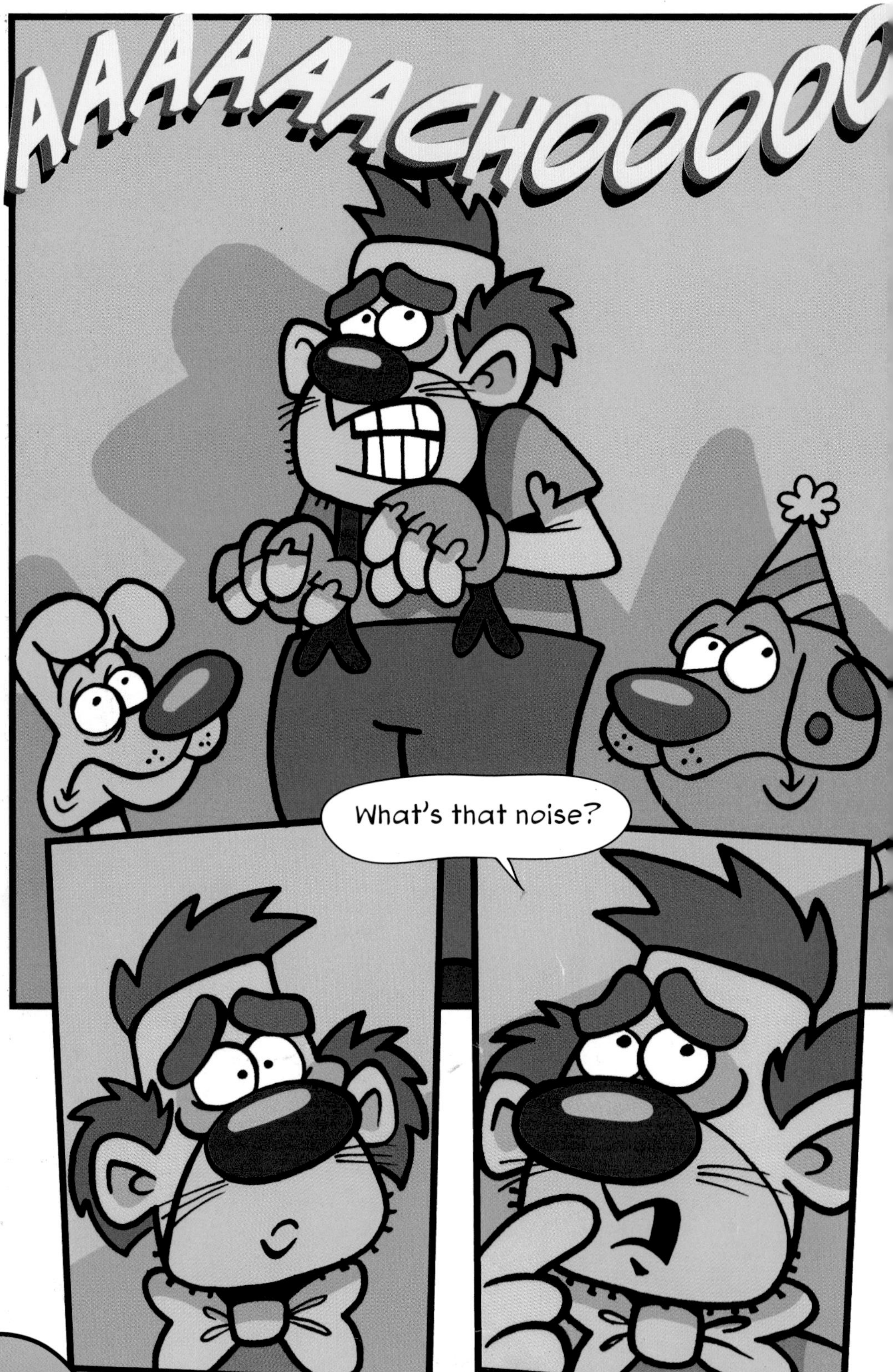
AAAAAACHOOOOO
What's that noise?

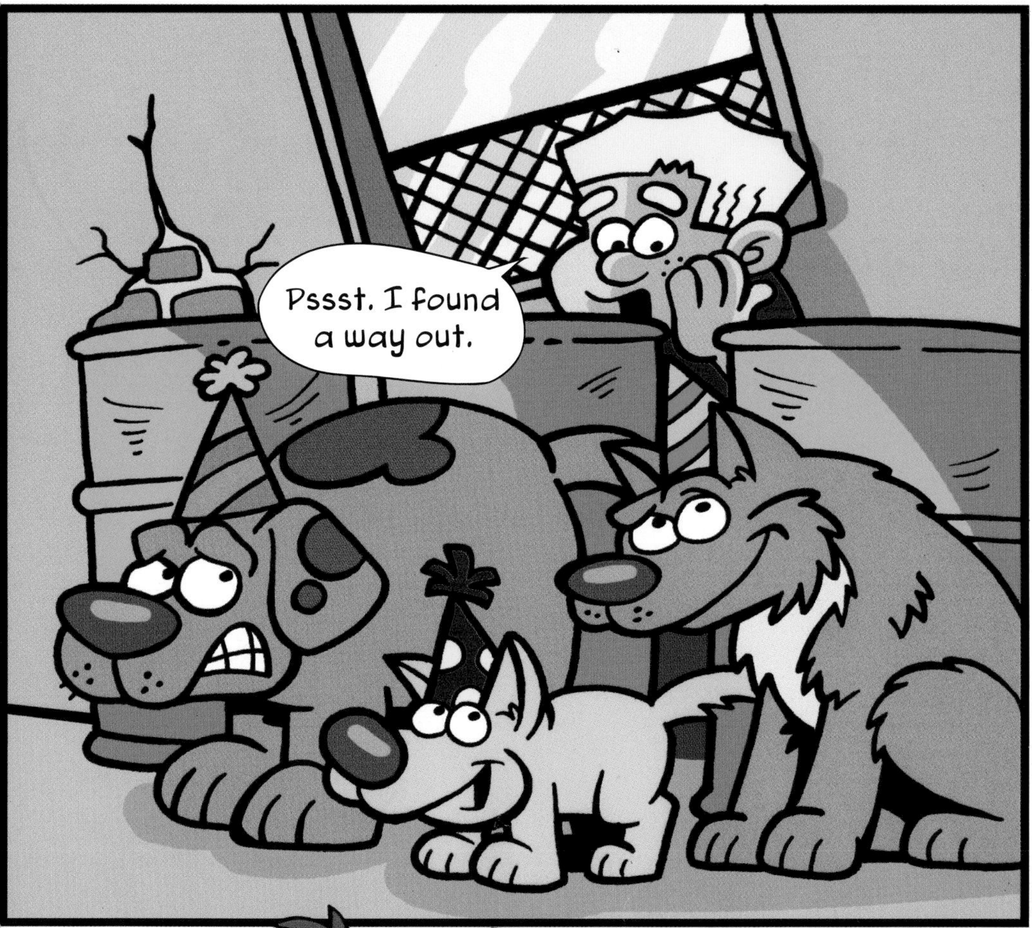
Pssst. I found a way out.

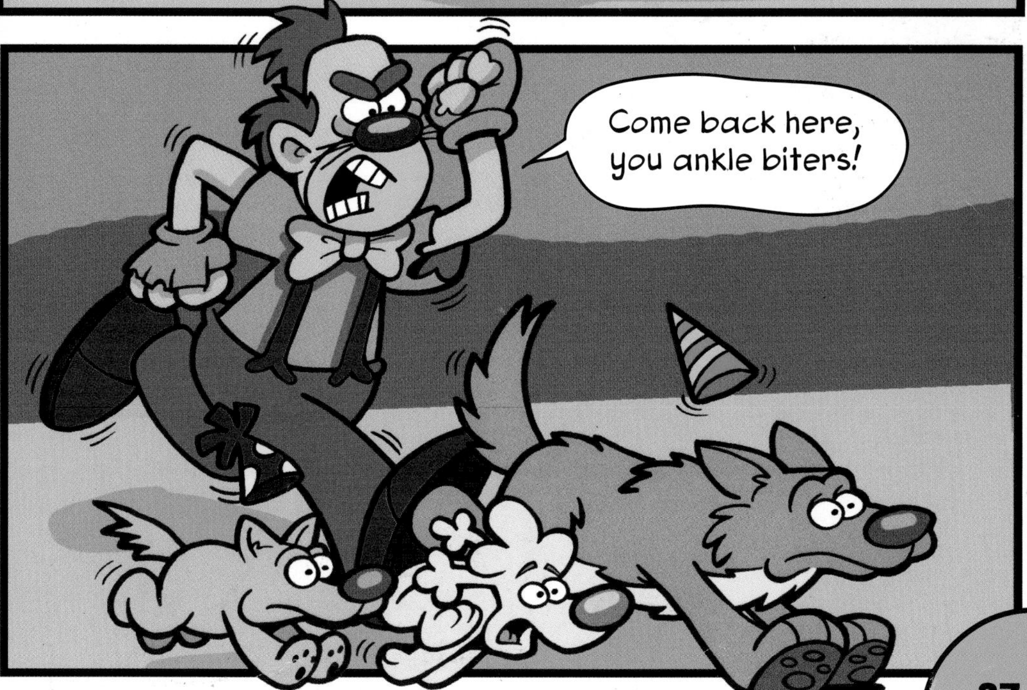
Come back here, you ankle biters!

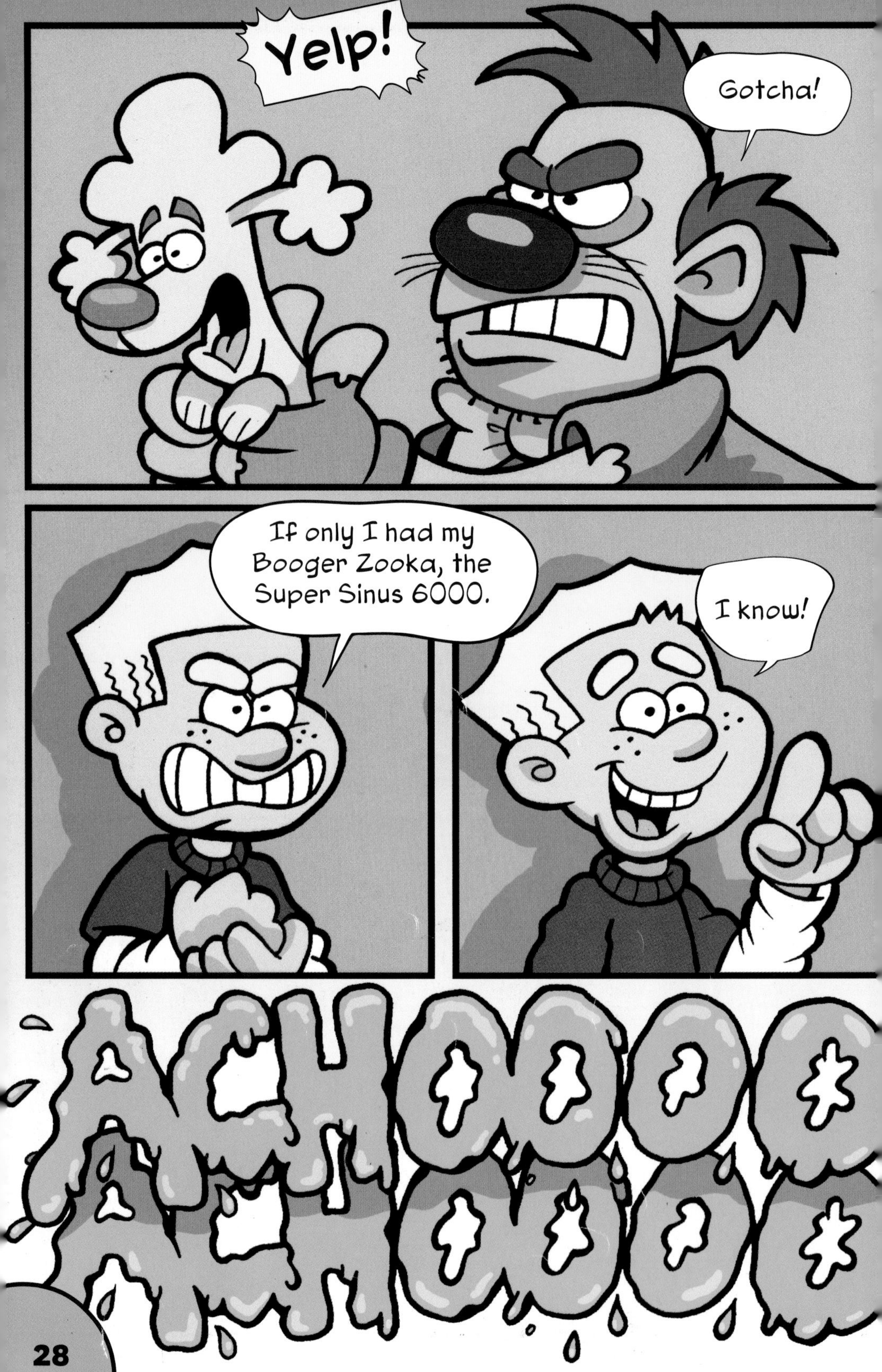
Yelp!
Gotcha!
If only I had my Booger Zooka, the Super Sinus 6000.
I know!
ACHOOO
ACHOOO

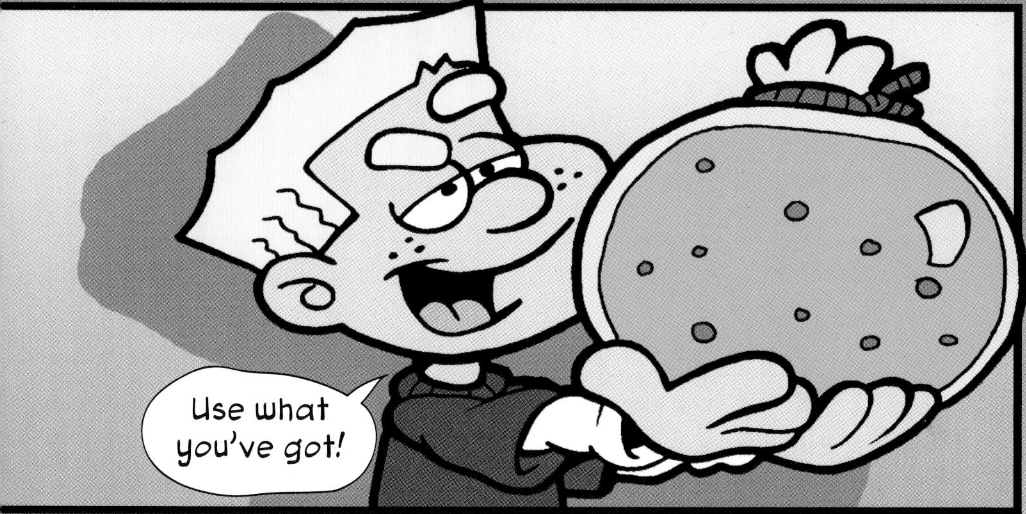
Use what you've got!

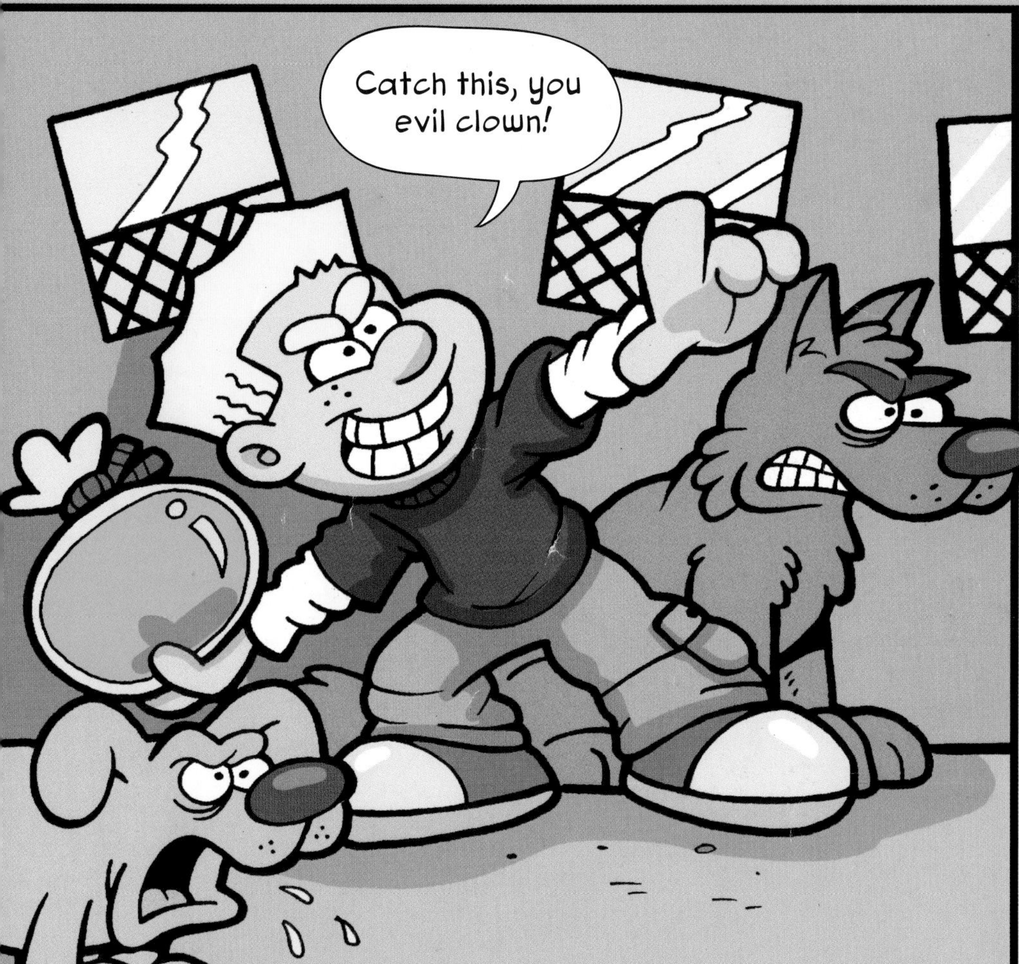
Catch this, you evil clown!

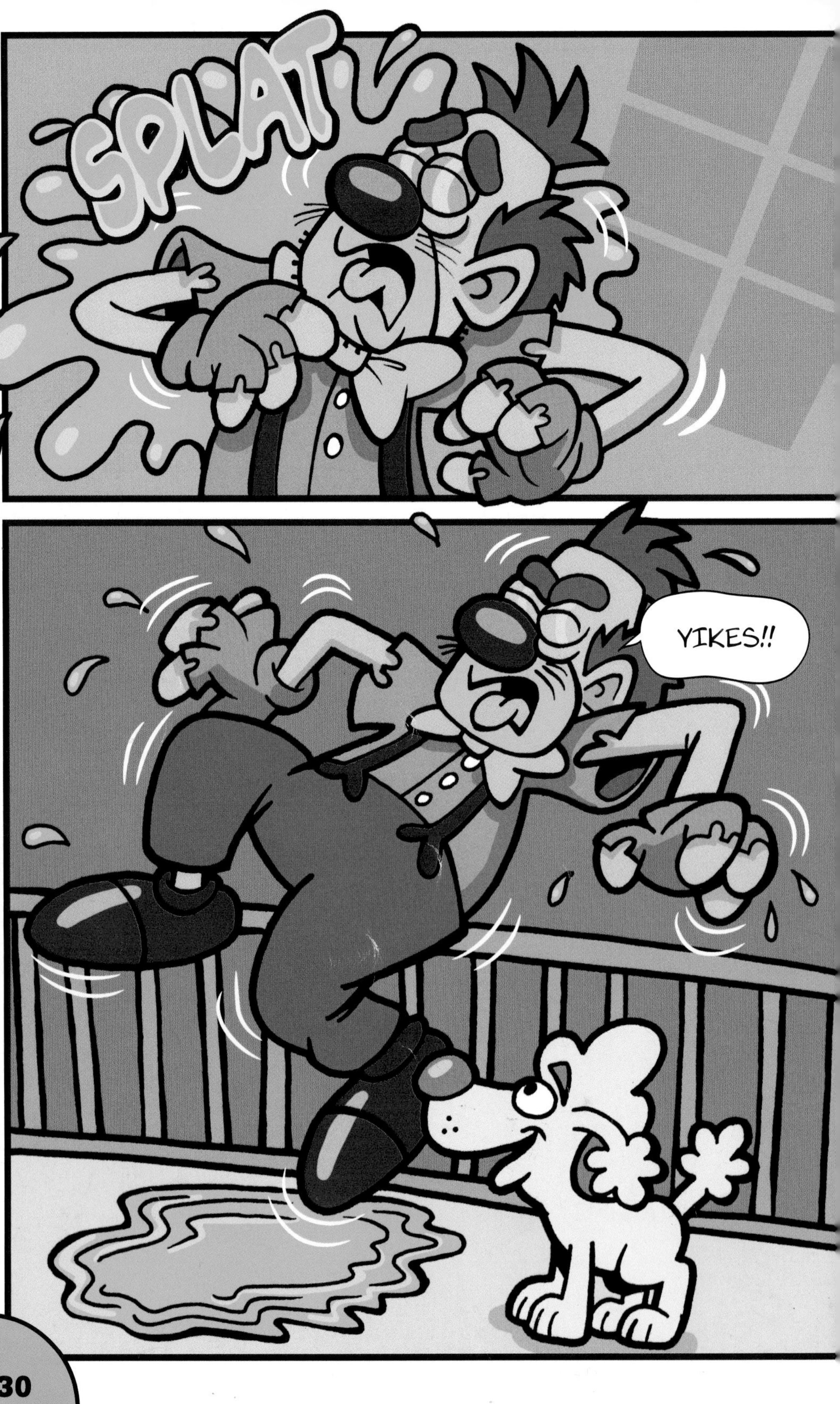
SPLAT
YIKES!!

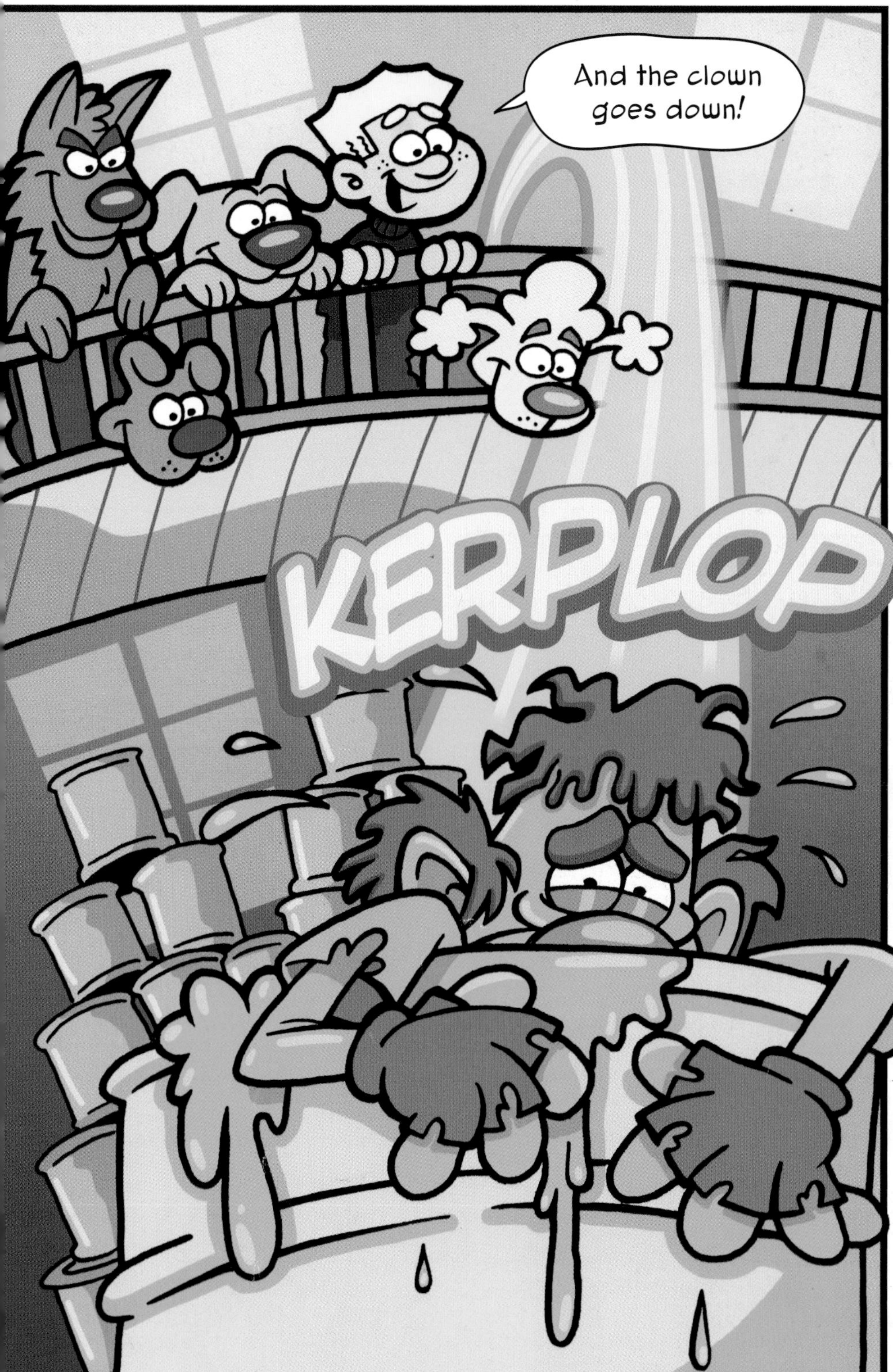
And the clown goes down!
KERPLOP

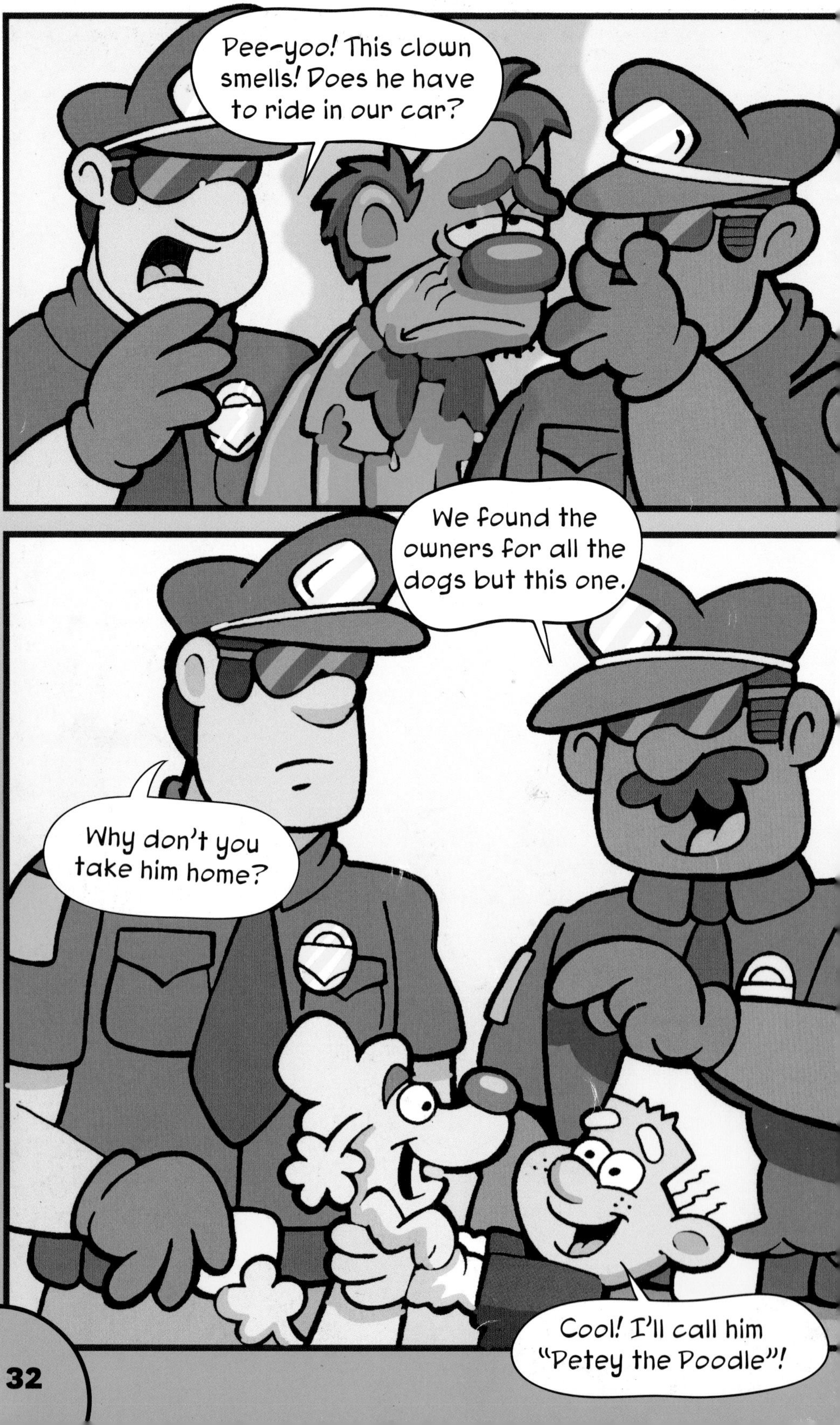
Pee-yoo! This clown smells! Does he have to ride in our car?
We found the owners for all the dogs but this one.
Why don't you take him home?
Cool! I'll call him "Petey the Poodle"!

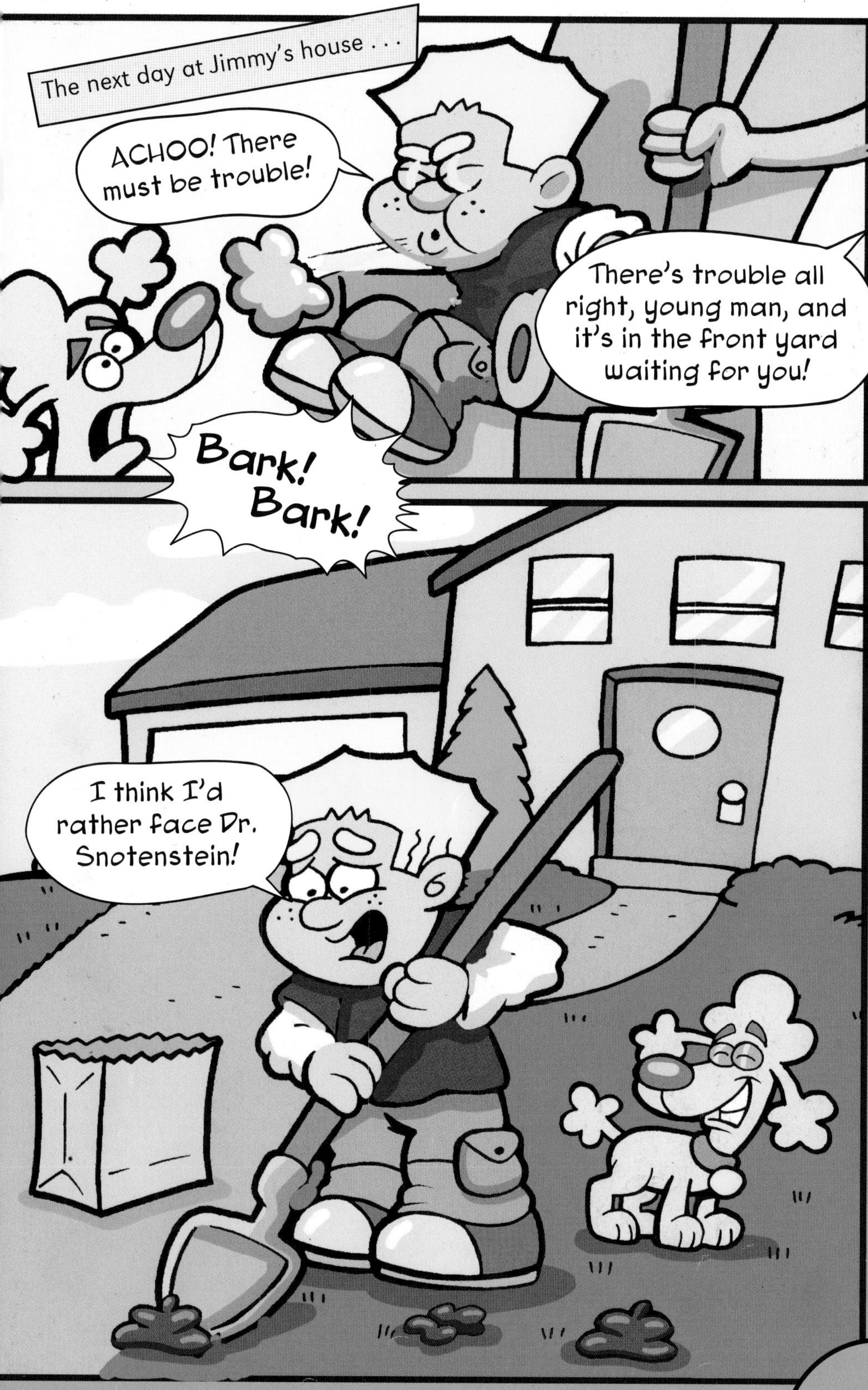
The next day at Jimmy's house . . .
ACHOO! There must be trouble!
There's trouble all right, young man, and it's in the front yard waiting for you!
Bark! Bark!
I think I'd rather face Dr. Snotenstein!

ABOUT THE AUTHOR

Born in 1962 in Denver, Colorado, Scott Nickel works by day at Paws, Inc., Jim Davis's famous Garfield studio, and he freelances by night. Burning the midnight oil, Scott has created hundreds of humorous greeting cards and written several children's books, short fiction for *Boys' Life* magazine, comic strips, and lots of really funny knock-knock jokes. He has also eaten a lot of midnight snacks. He was raised in Southern California, but in 1995 Scott moved to Indiana, where he currently lives with his wife, two sons, six cats, and several sea monkeys.

ABOUT THE ILLUSTRATOR

Steve Harpster has loved drawing funny cartoons, mean monsters, and goofy gadgets since he was able to pick up a pencil. In first grade, instead of writing a report about a dog-sled story set in Alaska, Steve made a comic book about it. He was worried the teacher might not like it, but she hung it up for all the kids in the class to see. "It taught me to take a chance and try something different," says Steve. Steve landed a job drawing funny pictures for books. He used to be an animator for Disney. Now, Steve lives in Columbus, Ohio, with his wonderful wife, Karen, and their sheepdog, Doodle.

GLOSSARY

harumph (har-UMF)—a noise adults make when you sneeze and forget to cover your mouth

mangy (MAYN-jee)—to be messy and have your hair in knots. Actually, it's the way you or your dog looks right before taking a bath.

sludge (sluj)—dirty, gloppy, mucky stuff

Super Sinus 6000 Booger Zooka (SOO-per SY-nuhss BOOG-er ZOO-ka)—the perfect weapon for loading and throwing snot at villains

tutus (TOO-toos)—short ballet skirts with too many ruffles. Girls like wearing these. Dogs do not.

CLOWN CLUES

Being a clown is serious business!

The biggest number of clowns ever gathered in one place at one time is 850. That's a lot of red noses!

The fear of clowns is known as coulrophobia (KOOL-roh-fo-bee-yuh).

Clowns consider it bad luck to use blue face paint.

The word *clown* comes from the word *clod*, which means "a clumsy person."

Clown Alley is the name of the area in a circus where clowns get dressed and put on their make-up.

Until 1998 there was an actual clown college. Graduates were guaranteed a job in the famous Barnum and Bailey Circus.

It can take a clown up to two hours to apply face make-up. Most clowns make sure that none of their real skin shows.

Most circuses are performed inside rings and are hosted by a ringmaster. That's because the first circuses were performed in ancient Rome in giant circular stadiums. "Circus" is the Roman word for "circle."

Why don't the circus lions eat the clowns? Because the clowns taste funny!

DISCUSSION QUESTIONS

1. When did you think that Mrs. Beasley was up to no good? What sort of clues did the writer give you?

2. Scurvy the Clown only wants to begin his own amazing dog circus. Does this really make him a villain?

3. If you were Jimmy, how would you have helped rescue the dogs from Mrs. Beasley and Scurvy the Clown?

ACHOOO!

WRITING PROMPTS

1. Jimmy's nose always alerts him to trouble.
   Do you have anything that alerts you to trouble?
   If so, what is it?

2. Oh no, someone new just moved in next door to you
   and they are up to something evil! What exactly are
   they up to, and how are you going to stop them?

3. There sure are a lot of sound effects in this story.
   That's one way writers make the story come to life.
   Describe how the story would be different if there
   were no sound effects. How else would you know
   what a Super Sinus 6000 sounded like? Take three
   pages with great sounds and replace them with
   sounds of your own.

INTERNET SITES

Do you want to know more about subjects related to this book? Or are you interested in learning about other topics? Then check out FactHound, a fun, easy way to find Internet sites.

Our investigative staff has already sniffed out great sites for you!

Here's how to use FactHound:

1. Visit *www.facthound.com*

2. Select your grade level.

3. To learn more about subjects related to this book, type in the book's ISBN number: **1598890530**.

4. Click the **Fetch It** button.

FactHound will fetch the best Internet sites for you!